## She … she w…

He must have read her mind, for suddenly he was there in front of her, pulling her into his arms in one smooth movement. For a moment she stood still, letting her body relax against his, abandoning herself to the wave of pleasure that washed over her.

For the first time in a long while she felt utterly safe and secure. She could have stayed in his arms for ever.

Then her practical, common-sense self took over, and she murmured breathlessly into his shirtfront, 'Jeremy, please, let me go. I don't want this.'

He nuzzled the top of her head and slowly loosened his arms, allowing her to draw away from him.

He said with husky tenderness, 'I wish to God that you did, my love. But I'm used to waiting for what I want to happen. I've spent a lifetime perfecting patience.'

**Margaret O'Neill** started scribbling at four and began nursing at twenty. She contracted TB and, when recovered, did her British Tuberculosis Association training before general training at the Royal Portsmouth Hospital. She married, had two children, and with her late husband she owned and managed several nursing homes. Now retired and living in Sussex, she still has many nursing contacts. Her husband would have been delighted to see her books in print.

# THE GENTLE TOUCH

BY

MARGARET O'NEILL

Harlequin Mills & Boon

Medical Romance

First Published 2001
First Australian Paperback Edition 2001
ISBN 0 733 52940 2



Published by
Harlequin Mills & Boon
3 Gibbes Street
CHATSWOOD NSW 2067
AUSTRALIA



Printed and bound in Australia by
McPherson's Printing Group

# CHAPTER ONE

ALEC MASTERSON looked up from the battered mess that was Trevor Black's face and glanced across at Veronica. 'Did you contact Mr Grant, Sister Lord?'

'I left a message for him with his secretary. She promised to locate him and pass on your request.'

Mr Masterson, the A and E consultant, grunted, and everyone worked in silence for several minutes. Then he glanced down the table to where a doctor and a nurse were bent over Trevor's legs. 'So what's your opinion on the fractured femur, Dr Ferguson? Do we need to resplint?' he asked.

'The emergency splints applied by the paramedics will hold till the patient goes up to the ward. It's a mid-shaft clean break and there's no bleeding into surrounding tissues.' Diana Ferguson, on her first rotation in A and E, spoke in a soft but firm voice. 'The other leg is bruised and there are a few lacerations, but none are deep—they only require cleaning up.'

'Right! We'll trust your diagnosis. No point in resplinting if it's not necessary. Better left to the orthopaedic chaps—they might want to put him in traction, or plaster him up straight away. We've a similar situation with the arm, a clean break in the shaft of the humerus, so we can concentrate on the face and head injuries. We can do something about the jaw pro tem, but I don't want to touch the other facial injuries until the plastic surgeon's had a look at them.'

He straightened up and lifted his shoulders to ease the

stiffness. 'Like to hazard a guess why that is, Diana?' He slanted the young doctor a quizzical glance.

Diana blushed and shook her head. It was the first time he had called her by her first name. Of all the staff she had worked with in her months at the hospital, Mr Masterson was the most formal and she was rather in awe of him. Everyone called him 'Mr Masterson', even the nurse manager, Veronica Lord.

Alec smiled, something he didn't do often. 'It's because I haven't got the expertise to put this lad's face together without leaving scarring. It needs an expert in reconstructive surgery. Even patching him up might cause further damage if we don't do it right, which is why, when we've finished cleaning him up, we're just going to place sterile dressings over the wounds and wait for Mr Grant...'

'You called, oh master?' asked a low, dry voice full of irony, from the doorway.

Masterson's head came up with a jerk and his thin-lipped mouth twitched again into a smile.

'Jeremy! Good of you to come.' He looked down at Trevor, who had stopped trying to talk through his swollen lips and had at last succumbed to the powerful analgesics he had been given, and was almost asleep. 'I want you to look at this poor lad. His motorcycle was in collision with a bus. The bus driver had a coronary attack, lost control and swerved in front of young Trevor. It was a head-on collision and the lad's face took the...'

Veronica didn't take in any more. She kept her head bent and her hands busy swabbing blood from a dozen tiny cuts on Trevor's forehead, ensuring that they were free of shards of metal or plastic from his shattered helmet. But her mind was seething, catapulting back over the years.

Jeremy Grant! Surely it couldn't be—not the Jeremy

Grant she had known. In the six weeks she had been at the Porthampton University Hospital, she had heard of Mr Grant, at thirty-two the youngest consultant in the hospital. For some reason she had never heard him referred to as Jeremy Grant. It was hearing the two names together that had rung bells. Just hearing of a Mr Grant would never in a thousand years made her think of the Jeremy Grant whom she hadn't seen or thought of since her school days.

Automatically Veronica disposed of the used swab and neatly picked up a fresh one with the forceps she was holding.

Mr Masterson motioned to her to stop and she moved back from the table as the two surgeons bent over the comatose patient and murmured together.

Jeremy Grant! Her thoughts winged down memory lane. Way back to a school play, *A Midsummer Night's Dream*, when she, a precocious thirteen-year-old, had played Titania and he at seventeen, tall, thin and lanky, his adolescent spots almost concealed beneath stage make-up, had played Oberon... For a second she closed her eyes and took several deep breaths before opening them and focusing on the bent heads of the two surgeons.

Both heads were dark, but Jeremy's hair was darker and thicker and cut well but flamboyantly; it was a little long so that it touched the collar of his white shirt which he wore with his conservative suit. And it was without the smattering of grey that speckled Alec Masterson's. Not surprising, he must be ten or fifteen years younger than the A and E boss.

She still found it hard to consider that it could be the Jeremy Grant she'd known at school. Somehow that Jeremy and this one just didn't match up. Although his age was about right and he was tall, something over six feet, she guessed. But how could that schoolboy Jeremy be the distinguished surgeon obviously admired by Alec Masterson?

His mother had been a widow or a single mum. How on earth could she have supported him through medical school? True, he'd been voted head boy by his peers as well as teaching staff in his last year at school, so apparently he'd had something going for him.

At thirteen, when looks had been paramount to her, she had thought this weird. It had been strange that in spite of his acne and a certain aloofness, arrogance even, he had been quite popular, at least with the boys.

The girls had all said, 'Shame about the spots.'

Without looking up, he suddenly shot his hand out across the table, palm upwards in the time-honoured gesture of all surgeons waiting for an instrument to be put into it. It made her jump.

'Forceps, please, Sister.' He half looked up then, his face at an angle. There was no pitting on the little she could see, but—

'Sister?' He sounded snappish.

Veronica picked up a pair of forceps from the trolley and placed them in his palm. Jeremy bent over Trevor again and delicately lifted the ragged flap of skin and muscle, which was all that remained of Trevor's cheek, and peered beneath it. He and Alec murmured again.

Jeremy spoke in a low but distinctive voice, the sort of voice that commanded attention. It was a voice Veronica remembered, the voice that had resonated round the stage and school hall all those years ago…

'Nerves and blood vessels relatively undamaged—should be able to put them together. All it needs now is a protective pad to hold it firm and prevent puckering and any further bleeding until I can get to it. The ear lobe, that can be stitched up. Done carefully, it won't need my sort of surgery. Nose and jaw need proper reconstruction work, but obviously will need some holding attention before that. I want him warded with me, Alec. I need to get cracking as soon as he's fit enough and that means twenty-four-hour nursing and observation care by my team. I can make a bed available later today.'

'The orthopaedic boys will want him for assessment.'

'No way, they haven't got the trained staff to observe my stuff. And surely if these are straightforward fractures they should be easy enough to deal with.' Jeremy straightened up. 'You can put that pad over the skin flap, Sister,' he said to Veronica. 'Nice and firm and flat, please, and dry dressings elsewhere when Mr Masterson's finished. Some of those smaller wounds may need a bit of grafting.'

'Yes, Mr Grant.' Veronica nodded without looking up. With steady fingers she swabbed the cheek clean, gently patted it dry and placed a large sterile protective pad over that side of his face, securing it with special tape that wouldn't pull the damaged skin too badly when it was removed.

The two surgeons continued to converse in low voices as she worked.

Then in a slightly raised voice, Alec said, 'I'll send him up to the trauma unit, Jeremy. That way both you and the orthopods can have access to him and the necessary X-rays can be done, and he'll have the special nursing care necessary. There's nothing to indicate brain damage but we need to make sure.' He produced another tiny quirk of the lips. 'Don't worry, old son, by this time tomorrow you'll have him safely installed on your own patch and will be able to get to work on him.'

Jeremy smiled cheerfully and raised an ironic eyebrow. 'I must be grateful for any crumbs from the rich man's table. Thanks for letting me have a look at him, Alec. You've certainly done him a favour. He's a nice-looking chap and we'll try to keep him that way.' And with a brisk 'Good morning' and a nod to include everyone, Jeremy Grant took himself off.

Everyone had to work flat out to keep pace with the incoming casualties. Several of the passengers in the bus had been injured, a few seriously, but none as seriously as Trevor or the driver.

In fact, the driver had died on the table in spite of high-powered resuscitation by the crash team. The staff involved with him had been subdued for a while. It always happened, however experienced the doctors and nurses were and however hard they had worked. There was always a whisper of regret and sadness, a niggling doubt as to whether they might have done more.

The waiting room remained chock-a-block all morning and any personal thoughts had to be pushed into the background. Although she had lapsed earlier whilst Jeremy Grant had been examining Trevor, Veronica normally found it easy enough to squash personal problems. She had long ago learned how to concentrate on the task in hand.

Without noticing, she worked through her lunch-hour, but by mid-afternoon, when the incoming stream of ambulances began to tail off, she decided to take a break. She was on a long day and not due off till nine. The evening was likely to be as busy as the morning had been so she must pace herself.

She tracked down Janice Porter, her senior staff nurse, who was attending to a small girl who'd fallen from a swing and sprained her wrist.

Veronica crouched down and smiled at the small girl

then turned to Janice. 'Will you hold the fort for me, Janice, please? I'm going off for an hour. Unless it's belting down, I'm going to take my sandwiches outside and soak up the sunshine and breathe in a few lungfuls of fresh air.'

'And petrol fumes and smoke from the incinerator and…'

'Hey, don't spoil my illusions. There's got to be a corner somewhere where I can sit and commune with nature.'

She didn't want to commune with nature: what she wanted to do was mull over and digest the possibility that Jeremy Grant, the distinguished consultant she had met this morning, was the Jeremy Grant she had known at school.

He couldn't be, could he? she asked herself as she collected her sandwiches and jacket from her office. The brief glimpse she'd had of a small portion of one side of his face as he'd examined Trevor had looked clean-shaven and smooth. Surely the severe acne the young Jeremy had had would have left some scarring—unless, of course, memory was exaggerating and he hadn't been so badly affected.

Veronica let herself out through a side door into a lawned and gravelled area where there were a few trees and shrubs and a couple of ancient wooden seats donated in memory of 'Doris Shepherd'. Who Doris Shepherd was remained a mystery, but Veronica was grateful to have somewhere to sit.

It wasn't an ideal place to ponder, as the courtyard was overlooked on all sides by corridor windows, but it was the nearest she was likely to find to seclusion. In the few weeks she had been at Porthampton, she had never seen anybody there.

The early March sun was shining and it was surprisingly warm, but there had been a recent shower and the bench seat was wet. She brushed off the worst of the raindrops and laid down her jacket, then sat herself down to eat and think. But a couple of mouthfuls of her sandwich and the warm sun shining on her face acted like a sedative and her eyelids drooped and then closed.

How long she'd dozed, dead to the world, she had no idea, and she wasn't roused by a sound but by a movement on the seat beside her. Her eyes flickered, then opened wide. She turned her head and found herself staring into a pair of blue-black eyes.

'Ah, sorry I woke you, proud Titania. You looked very peaceful, deep in the arms of Morpheus.'

*Titania!* Only the seventeen-year-old Jeremy Grant could have called her that. And the blue-black eyes could only belong to *that* Jeremy.

Veronica continued to gape at him, her eyes wide. Her mouth was also wide for a moment until she thought to close it. How could it be *that* Jeremy? Where were the scars that his teenage blemishes must have left? He couldn't possibly manage to conceal them beneath medicinal make-up at this close range, though in his position he would have access to the best.

Her hand went up instinctively to cover her own scar—the scar that marred her otherwise perfect beauty.

Jeremy closed his fingers lightly round her wrist before she reached her face. 'Tell me, Veronica, love, how did it happen?' he asked. 'And when?'

His voice was gentle but firm, and there was no surprise or curiosity in it at finding himself face to face with someone he hadn't seen for, what…?

It had been fifteen years ago when they'd appeared together in *A Midsummer Night's Dream*, for she'd been a cocky thirteen-year-old, full of herself and her looks, and he'd been a mature seventeen-year-old, tall and lanky and in her eyes totally unprepossessing except for his rich, resonant voice which had already broken, already mature. He'd had a maturity which had set him apart from the other boys and would have made him a target for the girls had it not been for his wretched acne.

Veronica, spoilt because of her beauty and intelligence, had despised him with all the vehemence that a thirteen-year-old could. Remembering the silly airs and graces she had used to make him aware of her dislike, she felt herself blushing, something that she rarely did.

He said softly, 'You're remembering, aren't you, Beauty and the Beast?'

She reddened still further and found her own voice at last. 'Don't,' she pleaded. 'What a horrid, spoilt creature I was. I can't think how you put up with me during those rehearsals.'

'Can't you?' Neither his midnight blue eyes nor dry tone gave anything away. 'Well, it wasn't a picnic for you either, was it?'

She recalled how she'd had to psych herself up before rehearsals to let him be close, and a little spurt of anger flared up. Even now she had difficulty suppressing a shudder… She shook her head. 'No, I couldn't bear your spots, but I shouldn't have been so cruel and unkind about them.'

He leaned forward and with his free hand smoothed a strand of hair, which had escaped the restraining comb, back behind her ear.

'Don't be so hard on yourself, love, you were only thirteen. I'm not surprised that you were repelled by them. As to why I put up with your obvious dislike, you were the school beauty. Nearly all my friends fancied you, although you were only in second year and small fry to us.

So did I for a while—fancy you, I mean. But you could have the pick of the guys and were unlikely to pick me.'

His chiselled lips lifted at the corners in a wry smile, 'Even though I had some clout as head boy. Playing opposite to you in ''The Dream'' seemed as good a way as any to get close to you—physically close. And, like any other healthy teenager, that's what I wanted.'

He's got a lovely mouth, Veronica thought, and wondered why she hadn't noticed it all those years ago. She realised that he was still holding her wrist, and gave her hand an experimental tug. His grip tightened slightly, holding her hand away from her face.

She didn't struggle, but darted a glance round the windows surrounding the courtyard. There were one or two people striding along the corridors, some with heads turned and looking toward the bench.

Deliberately demure, she murmured, 'Don't you mind being watched by all and sundry, a consultant in a compromising position with a humble nursing sister?'

He snorted. 'Humble? Dear Veronica, there's nothing humble about you. You walk like a queen and act like a queen, and I bet any of the male glances are purely of envy, because I've got the undivided attention of the most beautiful female in the hospital.'

To Jeremy's consternation and amazement, tears glittered in her smoky grey eyes and, instead of trying to pull her wrist from his grasp, Veronica thrust his hand hard against the side of her face, tracing the faint ridge that ran like a crescent from above her eyebrow, round her eye to her cheekbone.

'What, with this hideous thing? You don't have to try so hard to be nice, Jeremy, now that our roles are reversed. From what I've heard, it isn't your usual style. Do you know that you're sometimes referred to as being arrogant and woman-proof—?'

A deep, throaty laugh interrupted her. 'From some quarters,' he said, 'but I think you'll find that that description comes largely from female staff who…' His voice trailed off.

'Who had the temerity to try to form a relationship with you, or even a one-night stand? And you gave them an instant brush-off.' Veronica's voice was withering.

Jeremy said softly, 'Men get harassed, too, you know, it isn't all one-sided. But Veronica, believe me, when I said that you're the most beautiful woman in the hospital, I damn well meant it. You are that, scar and all.'

Veronica searched his face intently and seemed satisfied that he meant what he said.

'Thank you. And in all fairness, I should say that your reputation as a brilliant surgeon who is marvellous with his patients far outweighs the criticism. You must have given hope to so many people. Carry on with the good work, Jeremy. I dare say we'll bump into each other from time to time, but I must dash now.'

Jeremy didn't try to detain her, but watched her walk away from him with long, yet feminine strides and a straight, regal back.

A shoulder-length coil of red-gold hair—a kind of strawberry blonde—controlled by businesslike combs, gleamed in the sunlight. If she released her hair from the restraining combs, he mused, it would swing like a curtain round her face and conceal the scar—perhaps she did wear it like that when she was off duty.

There was no point in following her, he'd made contact. But he promised himself that he would make damned sure that they would bump into each other from time to frequent time. Not that he had any personal interest in her, his interest was solely professional—wasn't it? Of course it was. All he wanted to do was use his skills to help this still beautiful woman, who had once given him such a hard time, regain her flawless perfection, or as near as was possible.

That was what his job was all about, restoring damaged faces and helping to restore damaged personalities.

He had no personal axe to grind and was grateful to Alec for bringing the matter to his attention a few days before.

They had been lunching in the consultants' dining room.

'I have this new deputy nursing manager,' Alec had said. 'Beautiful woman, top-notch nurse, but she has a scar on her face, an old one by the look of it, though mostly it's hardly visible—she's clever with her make-up. She's very sensitive about it. Would you try and persuade her to let you take a look at it next time you come down to A and E? I know you're taking an interest in repairing old scar tissue.'

Jeremy looked at his friend and colleague sitting at the other side of the table. His face was as impassive as usual, but there was note in his voice that suggested an eagerness for Jeremy to see this woman. Was it significant? Was Alec belatedly becoming aware of the female sex after years in the wilderness? It didn't seem likely, but he was certainly very keen that he see this woman promptly.

'I'll see her in my clinic tomorrow. For you, Alec, I'll start a little earlier than usual.'

Alec had gone very still, staring down at his food, and then after several minutes said, 'She doesn't know that I've spoken to you and has never spoken of her scar. Sister Lord's a very private person, as far as I can see, everyone's friend but not especially friendly with anyone in particular. I'd rather make this casual. I wouldn't like her to think that my interest is in any way personal.'

Jeremy felt the hairs on the back of his neck rise.

'Lord, that's an unusual surname. I've only ever known one person named Lord, and that was in school aeons ago. A girl by the name of Veronica. But I can't see her in the role of a caring nurse, not her scene at all. She was a spoiled little brat, always the centre of attention, the boys were round her like bees round a honey pot.'

'Then she's changed,' said Alec abruptly. 'I think we can rule out there being two Veronica Lords. I'd like to bet we're both talking about the same woman, my new deputy manager.' He scored stripes with his fork on the starched tablecloth beside his plate. 'She's good, Jeremy, the best nurse manager I've ever had, great with the patients and junior staff, but she has this hang up about this scar—I think it's why she holds back from forming...'

He stabbed at the cloth. 'Let's say that for her sake I'd like to see if it's possible to restore her to her original flawless beauty, or as near as can be achieved. And for you, I imagine, it would be a challenge right up your street.'

Alec's pager buzzed then and he left the table and didn't return, leaving Jeremy to ponder over the revelation that a one-time rather unpleasant little girl had turned into a caring, warm-hearted woman.

That had been three days ago, three days in which he had steeled himself for a meeting with Veronica, without knowing when that might be. And when the call had come from Alec this morning to assess a patient, he'd still not been sure that he could face her.

It had taken him years to put behind him her stinging remarks about his spots and general unsavouriness. His only defence had been not to let her see how much they'd hurt, to pull out all the stops and throw his weight about as head boy. To use his natural authority to appear above and beyond the barbs she'd hurled at him.

But it had been those barbs, he thought wryly, and the general misery of those teenage years that had propelled him headlong into plastic surgery and a determination to help others with facial disfigurements.

He gave a grim little smile. In a way, he had Veronica Lord to thank for the successful surgeon that he now was.

Jeremy got up from the bench and, head down, deep in thought, strolled to the door into the corridor, thrusting it open and walking through without looking up. Two nurses skipped out of his way with apologies, and he lifted his head and stared at them unseeingly for a moment, then went on his way to his office.

The nurses looked meaningfully at each other and raised their eyebrows.

'Is he really woman-proof?' muttered one.

'Or simply choosy?' suggested the other. 'I wouldn't mind giving him a whirl. Wish I knew a bit more about him.'

'Well, good luck to you, but he keeps his private life well under wraps. No one can get near him, though his team think he's the best thing since penicillin.'

The phone was ringing when Jeremy, still deep in thought, got back to his office. Before he'd picked it up some sixth sense told him that it was Alec calling.

'Glad to see that you've made contact.' he said when Jeremy lifted the receiver. 'I saw you in the courtyard with the delectable Miss Lord. Was there anything about her to remind you of the younger Veronica?'

'Not a lot, except that she's still got plenty of spirit. *If* I can ever persuade her to consider surgery, that will stand her in good stead. I should say that she's one gutsy lady and has turned out a hundred times better person than I would have expected.'

'I know that your powers of persuasion where your work's concerned are pretty well a hundred per cent, so get cracking, there's a good chap. She's the head of my team and deserves the best.' His receiver went down, cutting off the call.

Fleetingly, Jeremy wondered if Alec had any personal involvement with Veronica, and instantly dismissed the possibility. Alec was a bachelor through and through. He was simply a man who, beneath a steely exterior, concealed a heart of gold.

Jeremy looked at his watch—it was almost time for his ward round. Alec wanted him to use his powers of persuasion on Veronica Lord to let him examine her and at least give an opinion. Could he do it, should he do it? Her words—'role reversal'—popped into his mind.

Every patient he had ever operated on had been supersensitive and afraid of being patronised. Facial disfigurements, whether someone was born with them or acquired them later in life, did dreadful damage to the suffer's self-esteem. He walked a tightrope every time he treated a patient.

In Veronica's case, it would be worse because he had known her at her most beautiful when he had been a figure of derision. As he had expressed it—Beauty and the Beast, a beast who in the best pantomime tradition had been sadly lacking in confidence, though he'd put on a good show of indifference. Now she, the one-time beauty, was herself vulnerable, and he no longer needed to bolster his confidence by bowling over every attractive woman who came his way.

He'd gone down that route years ago, once he'd been free of the blemishes that had plagued his teens and had become a sought-after bachelor. His lankiness had given way to broad shoulders and firm muscles. In his precious free time he swam and played squash and the occasional round of golf with Alec.

But how was any of that going to help him get close enough to Veronica to persuade her to let him her examine her scar properly? Patience would have to be the name of the game. Well, he had bucketsful of that where his work was concerned.

He was flooded with sudden confidence and a tingle of awareness ran through him. Somehow he *would* persuade Veronica to accept his help without making her feel patronised.

He picked up his stethoscope, stuffed it in his pocket and strode through to the outer office.

His secretary was busy tapping away at her keyboard. He smiled at her. 'Come on, Maude, let's be having you. I'm off to do my round.'

## CHAPTER TWO

VERONICA returned to the department with her mind an absolute maelstrom of troubled thoughts. She wished that she had time to marshal them into some sort of order so that she could tidy them away and then get on with her life.

Her talk with Jeremy Grant had thoroughly unsettled her and she wanted to forget that he was at work somewhere in this vast hospital and might bob up at any minute. But, as always, time was at a premium from the moment she returned to duty.

The waiting room was nearly as full as earlier in the day. There had been a series of small traffic accidents almost on their doorstep, one collision leading to another. Not surprising since the busiest road in the city passed a hundred yards from the main entrance.

Most of the accident cases weren't serious. The bumper-to-bumper traffic had been moving too slowly on the wet, slippery road to cause major injuries. There were cuts and abrasions needing a few stitches, but even those with minor injuries had to be given anti-tetanus injections, and they were time-consuming. And another time-consuming job was to reassure those suffering from shock, and almost everyone was to some degree.

'For shock,' Alec Masterson constantly reminded his staff, 'can be a killer, don't forget that.'

Three whiplash cases were sent to X-Ray for investigation to establish whether or not there was spinal or other damage, and there were a few broken bones to be given priority and whisked off for X-rays. But no one was haemorrhaging to death or deeply unconscious. The triage nurse, whose job it was to sort out the seriously injured from those less hurt, had no difficulty in applying the priorities of the checklist that Alec Masterson insisted on every member of staff knowing off by heart—breathing, bleeding, broken bones, babies.

It was, thought Veronica, a nice, simple way of prioritising when you were snowed under with bodies.

Interspersed with the RTA cases, the constant procession of ambulances were bringing in the usual trickle of emergencies from domestic calls, but none of them so far had been life-threatening.

In other words, thought Veronica, doing a whirlwind check of the cubicles to see that everything was going smoothly, it's a typical day in A and E—under pressure. We'll cope, we always do, but it'll be all hands to the pump. We could do with many more pairs of hands but, with the usual economic restrictions applying, that was probably wishful thinking.

Stifling these familiar, unpalatable thoughts, she went through to the waiting room—noisy with chatter, crying or boisterous children, coughing and shuffling, and shrilling telephones. She stopped for a moment to scoop up a toddler hell-bent on evading his mother, and restored him to the exhausted, obviously pregnant woman.

'Thanks.' The woman sank back onto the seat and struggled to hold the wriggling child on her lap. 'You wouldn't believe that he's been throwing up and coughing half the night and most of the day, would you?' she asked Veronica.

'Oh, but I would,' said Veronica with a smile. She'd done a spell in Paediatrics before she'd plumped for specialising in A and E. 'Why didn't you ask your GP to visit you? I'm sure he would have under the circumstances.' She glanced down at the give-away 'bump'. 'When's it due?'

'Six weeks' time,' puffed the woman. 'We've only just moved into the area and I haven't even registered with anyone yet. I'm going to do that on my way home later if the surgery's still open.'

If you can hang on that long, thought Veronica. Junior looks pretty imminent to me. She looked at the toddler's orange priority card with the number twenty printed on it. The information board on the wall gave the last child number being examined as ten.

'I'll go and see if we can hurry things up for you,' she said. 'What's the little one's name?'

'Kenny, Kenny Waldron.'

Veronica made her way over to the reception desk.

Rebecca, the senior receptionist, was wiping her perspiring face with a tissue. 'We've just had a red alert in,' she told Veronica. 'An old lady, partially blind, was knocked down on a crossing up near the bypass. She's critical, with multiple injuries. And the driver of the car that knocked her down is in shock and will be coming in, too. Can you believe people overtaking on a crossing?' She wiped her face again.

Veronica leaned across the desk and squeezed the receptionist's arm. 'Sorry about the hot flushes. It must be hell in here with the temperature that we have to keep the place. Have you started your HRT yet?'

'Yep, a couple of days ago. Thanks for pushing me to see my GP, he was most sympathetic.'

'They usually are,' said Veronica. 'Now, I'm away before I have the big bad boss on my tail for wasting time when the waiting room's full. I'll have a line through to my office, please, Rebecca, and I'll try to rustle up some more nurses. Oh, by the way…' She turned back. 'There's a small boy waiting to be seen, Kenny Waldron, number twenty. Can you push him forward a bit? He's not too bad, but his mum's heavily pregnant and you might end up with three patients if she has to wait much longer.'

The big bad boss, Alec Masterson, was waiting for Veronica in her office, examining her staff rota. He wasn't, in fact, all that big, not much taller than her five feet seven—five-nine perhaps, and slightly built—and bad was the wrong adjective. Stern, tough, grim, mostly unsmiling, he didn't tolerate fools and worked his team of medics almost to a standstill, especially the young house officers on the first rung of the medical ladder.

But he was forgiven for all this because as one young houseman had remarked, 'You know absolutely where you are with him and can trust him implicitly, even though he's like the tin man and hasn't got a heart. And, as a by-the-way, he happens to be a brilliant surgeon.'

After working with the formidable Alec for six weeks, Veronica thought that this was probably not true either. Brilliant surgeon and medic, yes, but not the bit about his heart. Mr Masterson had got a heart, he just kept it well hidden. She recalled the look of compassion in his eyes this morning when he'd examined the young motorcyclist's face. He had a heart all right.

Personally she liked working with him. He never interfered with the way she organised her nursing staff, but approached her upfront if he thought something was wrong.

He looked round as she entered the office.

'Getting a briefing from Rebecca?' he asked in his staccato bark.

'I was,' replied Veronica with her usual cool. 'I know

we're getting an RTA in, an elderly lady knocked down on the bypass and the driver responsible. I'm just about to call Admin for permission to pull in some extra pairs of hands. I can't afford to take any nurses from out there—in fact, they need boosting.' She nodded in the general direction of the waiting room and cubicles. 'They're barely holding their own and waiting time's already over an hour. And your two medics are only just about coping, too.'

'That's Dick Shepherd and the new young doctor, Diana Ferguson, isn't it?'

Veronica nodded. 'She's doing well, in spite of the relentless pressure of one patient after another, even though most of their injuries are slight.'

'Tougher than being thrown in at the deep end as she was this morning, assisting with the motorcyclist? She looked as if she might pass out.'

'Yes, definitely. Then she had a personal fear to overcome and once she conquered it she could concentrate on obeying your instructions. Attending to an endless stream of patients requires stamina, and since she's been on duty for eighteen hours I guess she's running a bit short on reserves.'

Masterson's bleeper buzzed. He reached for the phone on Veronica's desk and barked into it.

He put the phone down a short time later, looking grim. 'There's another red alert—an accident in the docks. We'd better get cracking, Sister.' He turned about smartly and exited through the door.

It was after eleven when she went off duty and mumbled a tired goodnight to the security guard who let her out of the building. The adrenaline that had kept her going for the last few hours had suddenly drained away and she felt that her knees might buckle as she crossed the brightly lit staff car park.

She fished in her shoulder-bag for her car keys as she got near her little Fiat, and was within a few yards of it when the door of the car next to hers opened and a tall figure emerged.

'Oh!' The word came out on a rush of air. Veronica stopped in her tracks and her hand went to her throat. Her heart gave a terrific jolt. 'It's you.' She inhaled noisily. 'What are you doing here? Why aren't you parked in the consultants' car park? You gave me one helluva fright.'

'Sorry about that,' said Jeremy. 'Didn't mean to frighten you. After all, it's well lit.' He waved a hand round the almost empty car park. 'As to why I'm here, that must be obvious. I'm waiting for you.'

*He was waiting for her!* It didn't make sense, it wasn't obvious at all. They'd only met briefly today—or rather, met again—and he hadn't attempted to arrange another meeting when she'd walked away from him. Veronica made her legs move toward the Fiat, keys at the ready.

Jeremy moved between her and the driver's door. 'Look, suggestion to make—why not leave your car here and collect it tomorrow? I'll drive you home, Veronica, you're too whacked to drive yourself.'

'Don't be silly,' she said sharply. 'I often drive home after a long tour of duty—tonight is nothing new.'

He sighed heavily in what was probably exasperation—or perhaps it wasn't. For although he was so close, she couldn't see any expression in his inky blue-black eyes, in spite of the brilliantly lit park and a spectacularly large moon adding to the illumination.

'No, there's nothing new about work,' he agreed, 'but what is new is the emotional strain of today. Add that to physical tiredness and your driving skills are likely to be affected. Come on, Veronica, please, don't choose this moment to go all regal and distant with me.'

'I don't know what you mean.'

In fact, she did. It had been a traumatic sort of day, dealing with poor, battered Trevor, so young and good-looking, fearing for his future with scars much worse than her own. Then the shock of meeting Jeremy and having to come to terms with their differing roles. And, of course, the death of the bus driver in the next cubicle, the sudden silence when the crash team had stopped trying to resuscitate him.

To her fury, Veronica felt herself swaying. She really was exhausted.

Jeremy caught her by the shoulders. He said softly, 'Let me take you home, Veronica. No strings. I'll simply see you to your door.'

She nodded wordlessly.

He steered her to the Range Rover, dwarfing her little Fiat, and helped her into the passenger seat.

'I live…' she started to say.

'I know where you live,' he said briskly. 'In one of the houses owned by the trust for letting out to senior staff—Heatherington House. It's north of the town on Porthampton Hill. Now, stop talking and close your eyes till we get there.'

'Don't be so pat…'

She slept till they stopped on the drive outside Heatherington House, high on the hill overlooking Porthampton. Jeremy was looking down at her, his face enigmatic in the light from the porch. He hadn't switched on the courtesy light in the car.

'Thanks.' She fought off a feeling of disorientation and an extraordinary desire to kiss him full on his lovely mouth, and instead mumbled again, 'Thanks.' She fumbled with her seat belt until Jeremy leaned over and released it.

'Stay there,' he ordered, and slid out of his door and strode round to open hers. She couldn't believe how shaky her legs were and was glad to lean against him for support. 'Let me have your keys,' he said as they reached the door.

A tiny scrap of remaining pride made her open her mouth to protest but, anticipating this, he said impatiently, 'Please, don't argue, Veronica. You can hardly stand, woman.'

She handed over the keys, one for the outer door, one for her flat door. He keyed in the number printed on the tag and the door clicked open.

She made a hash of the stairs. 'Feels like climbing Everest,' she mumbled, as Jeremy half carried her from step to step.

'When did you last eat or drink?' Jeremy asked as he opened the door to her flat.

'This afternoon, I think. I went for a coffee during the evening but something stopped me before I could make it.'

The door to the kitchen was open. Jeremy pushed her gently into an armchair and without a word disappeared into the kitchen. She heard doors opening and shutting and the kettle being plugged in. Make yourself at home, why don't you? her tired mind muttered.

He reappeared a moment later. He was stirring something into what looked like a glass of sparkling mineral water.

'Drink that,' he said, pushing the glass into her hand.

'What is it?'

'Arsenic, what else? Please, just drink it, Veronica. It's only mineral water, honey and a pinch of salt. You're dehydrated and low on blood sugar and on the point of passing out. I've put the kettle on so we can have a cup of tea when you've finished that, and then, my love, it's bed for you. I'll pick you up in the morning. You're on at seven, aren't you?'

Veronica could only nod. He's like a general, marshalling his forces, she thought, her tired mind working overtime. A young, handsome general—a Roman general with his aquiline nose. Bet he's got great legs. They'd look stunning under a toga. Funny how he's turned out so handsome. Holding back an hysterical giggle, she took a sip of her drink and shuddered.

'It's medicine, drink it down like a good girl,' Jeremy said softly as he made for the kitchen.

He stayed for twenty minutes while she drank her tea, ate some biscuits and, at his insistence, got ready for bed. Wrapped in a mid-calf towelling dressing-gown that had seen better days, she saw him out of the flat.

'See you at six-thirty,' he said, as she closed the door and locked it behind him.

She leaned against the door listening to his footsteps as he walked toward the stairs. 'Oh, dear,' she murmured to the empty room, 'I forgot to thank him for…for everything.'

'Did you have a good night?' Jeremy asked Veronica when he picked her up at six-thirty the next morning. 'I must say, that considering the state you were in last night, you seem very bright-eyed and bushy-tailed this morning.'

The words, a favourite expression of his mother's, were very apt, he thought, with her mane of strawberry blonde hair, even caught back as it was in restraining combs. It glowed in the rosy dawn of a fine March morning. And her lovely profile with that slightly retroussé nose, and her complexion all peaches and cream, she looked to him as gorgeous as she'd ever done.

The scar was nothing. Add to all this beauty the caring, loving, intelligent qualities she had acquired since she'd been a spoilt schoolgirl, and no wonder she had aroused Alec's interest.

'I had a wonderful night,' Veronica said serenely. 'And that's thanks to you, Jeremy. Are you sure that you didn't lace my tea with something?'

Suddenly she was back on her usual form, the competent, forceful manager of a large department. She slanted him a bewitching smile.

His mouth twitched at the corners. He shook his head. 'Scout's honour.' He sketched a salute. 'You were simply exhausted emotionally and physically.'

'That's true.' She turned her head to look at him, and said softly, 'Jeremy, why don't you smile more often?'

The knuckles of his hands whitened as he gripped the steering-wheel. He drove in silence for a few minutes and Veronica wished that she'd held her tongue. It was too personal a thing to say to this man who in the hospital hierarchy was way above her, even in today's freer atmosphere where first-name terms were quite the norm. There were dozens of subtle unwritten rules to be adhered to.

The fact that they were old 'friends,' which was stretching it a bit considering the antipathy there had been between them in their schooldays, it didn't really entitle her to make comments like that, especially on such a short reacquaintanceship. She would have to apologise.

'I'm sorry. I shouldn't have said that, it was rude of me.'

He took his eyes off the road for a moment to glance at her. 'No, it wasn't. Surely the fact that we're old friends entitles you to make an honest comment.' There was no inflection, no sarcasm in his voice when he uttered the word 'friends'.

They were in the thick of the traffic now in the centre of the city, and then they were turning into the hospital drive and heading for the staff car park.

Veronica put a hand on his arm. 'Jeremy, stop here and let me get out, please. I'd just as soon that the world and his wife didn't see us arriving together. Tongues will wag.'

'After our meeting in the courtyard yesterday, I'm sure that tongues are already wagging. I told you then that I didn't mind, and I still don't.'

'But *I* do,' she said fiercely. 'I've only been here a few weeks and I'm still building my reputation. I don't care on a personal level, but I will not let *anything* affect my professional status—that's precious to me. And there's a difference between sitting in full view of everyone in the middle of the afternoon and arriving early in the morning in the same car. People will think…'

'That we've spent the night together… I wish.' His lips more than twitched this time, they curved into a real smile and his dark eyes gleamed—mockingly, she suspected.

Veronica's hand went up to cover her scar and her cheeks burned. Her heart felt like lead. She said bitterly. 'No, you're right to smile. Of course no one's going to suspect that you would want to sleep with a disfigured woman.'

Abruptly Jeremy pulled onto the grass verge and stopped. He released his seat belt and turned to look at her in obvious amazement.

'Veronica, you don't really think that, do you? That I of all people would make a bad joke of something like that? I know you're sensitive about your scar, I've never yet met a patient who isn't conscious of being scarred—

feeling different. Scars never just go skin deep, they go through to the soul. It's obviously an old scar, but I didn't know you were suffering quite so acutely, though Alec did warn me.'

'Alec!' It was Veronica's turn to be amazed. 'Do you mean Mr Masterson?'

'Yes,' Jeremy said tersely, 'though I shouldn't have told you that. I've broken a confidence, and I'm not in the habit of doing that.'

Veronica frowned. 'But why should Alec Masterson mention my scar to you? He's hardly ever noticed me except in a professional context, and certainly hasn't indicated that he's even noticed my scar.'

A car whizzed up the drive and the driver hooted as he—or she—passed.

'You were right,' Jeremy said. 'It is a bit too public here. Let's continue this conversation later. Have dinner with me tonight, Veronica.'

'Dinner?' She looked at him as if he were talking in a foreign language.

'Please. There's a nice pub not far from where I live, with a restaurant that serves a really decent meal where we could eat and talk.'

'Talk,' she repeated like a zombie. 'Jeremy, what did you mean about Alec Masterson and my scar?'

'That's what we'll talk about tonight.' His voice, which minutes before had been warm with concern, was suddenly clipped and dismissive. 'Now is not the time or place. I'll pick you up at seven.'

He watched her face as all sorts of expressions flickered across it. Oh, hell, he'd made a right mess of this morning. And that, he told himself grimly, is because you're letting your feelings take over, letting things become personal. You're slipping, man.

Perhaps she would refuse, tell him to take a running jump and leave her alone. Perhaps that would be the best solution all round. He wouldn't have to get further involved with her on a personal or professional basis. That's right, you chicken out, no matter that you are the only guy around who can help her, he jeered at himself.

Veronica's cool voice cut across his thoughts. 'If you stop ordering me around and ask nicely, you can pick me up at seven-thirty,' she said. 'Now, if you please, drop me off at the staff entrance and I'll be in time to take over from the night sister.'

He turned on the ignition. 'The staff entrance! I thought that you wanted to avoid wagging tongues.'

She gave him what he interpreted as a Mona Lisa-like smile, a smile from a woman of the world who had all the answers. It made him feel like the spotty teenage youth who'd adored her from afar, but had worked hard at not letting it show.

By the end of the rehearsals for *A Midsummer Night's Dream* he'd no longer fancied her, her childish behaviour had been a turn-off—well almost. Hearing one of the teaching staff refer to her as 'a spoilt little madam'—had helped him come to his senses.

But she was no longer a spoilt little madam, she was a beautiful, serene and caring woman with a scar that bothered no one but herself.

Jeremy glanced at her again before pulling slowly off the grass verge. His boyhood passion for her had died fairly painlessly, but he was conscious that the feelings that were overwhelming him now wouldn't be denied so easily.

Veronica said softly, the smile still playing round her lips, 'As you said, Jeremy, tongues will already be wagging. I guess I can ride them out.'

* * *

A and E didn't look or sound much different to the way it had last night when she'd gone off duty.

The waiting room was still pretty full and there was a red alert on its way in from a domestic accident.

'Not sure whether the injured party was pushed or fell down the stairs,' said Dick Shepherd, the registrar, who met her as she came out of her office. 'And her husband—boyfriend, whatever—isn't saying. According to Steve and Tess, the paramedics, he's in a pretty bad way as well so they've brought him in. He's obviously been in a fight and has what look like superficial stab or knife wounds, but whether the fight was with her or somebody else they don't know. And to add to the problem there's an infant involved, a little girl about a year old...'

Veronica grinned at the young registrar. 'So they're bringing her in, too,' said Veronica dryly. 'Oh, well, it never rains but it pours. Let's get cracking. The place will be crawling with police officers in no time flat.'

The day proceeded as most days did, with major emergencies interlaced with minor problems. Another cardiac arrest, similar to the bus driver's of the previous day, was admitted at midday.

'He didn't appear to be breathing when we arrived and pulse was non-existent, but he responded to a shot of adrenaline, external heart massage and oxygen,' Steve panted as they rushed to the resuscitation room. 'Pulse low and thready and swinging blood pressure, but there's been some general improvement.'

Bob Standish, the registrar in charge of the cardiac team, took over and intubated him to improve his breathing, while the nurses connected him up to the monitors and began undressing him, working round Bob and the house officer assisting. Everyone worked feverishly and skillfully, instantly obeying Bob's commands. No way were they going to have a repeat of yesterday's disaster if they could help it.

Things quieted down at about one o'clock and Veronica stopped for a quick lunch-break, even though she was only on till three. She was determined not to let her blood sugar drop as she had the previous day.

There was no chance of going outside as the rain was bucketing down, so she ate in her office. There was, as always, a pile of paperwork to be done: statistical reports on the number and type of injuries they had dealt with that week; a progress chart to complete for one of the nurses who was moving to another department at the end of the week, and a half-completed requisition form for stores.

She ignored them all—poured a coffee from the flask she had brought with her, unwrapped her sandwiches, kicked off her shoes and rested her feet on the second chair opposite her swivel, desk chair and heaved a huge sigh of relief.

'Nurses—' she could hear in her mind the voice of the elderly tutor at the beginning of her training ''—must take care of their feet. Never stand when they can sit and never sit when they can lie. They must learn the art of catnapping—that way they may last the course.'

How right she was, thought Veronica, taking a bite from her egg and cress sandwich.

For a few minutes she let her mind go blank, another bit of advice from Sister Halliday. Empty your mind, she'd advised, before tackling a new problem. That, too, had been good advice and over the years Veronica had become adept at this little exercise.

And that was how Alec Masterson found her a few minutes later when he knocked and, without waiting for an answer, entered her room in one smooth movement, as he usually did. Her eyes were closed, her mouth was full and her mind was empty—so empty that his brief knock hadn't registered. He stood and watched her as her neat jaw worked rhythmically as she chewed at her sandwich.

He smiled and turned and tiptoed from the room, closing the door quietly behind him.

## CHAPTER THREE

FOR once, Veronica was actually pleased to be going off duty, not because she was overtired and exhausted, as she'd been yesterday—her seven-to-three tour of duty today had been a doddle by comparison—but because she was anticipating having dinner tonight with Jeremy and clearing up the mystery of Alec Masterson's interest in her scar.

Her feelings were mixed and tumultuous. She had butterflies in her stomach as if she were going on her first date. Should she dress up for Jeremy? Pile on the make-up so that her scar was virtually invisible? For what? her sensible self asked. He knew all about her scar. Perhaps she should be casual.

Whatever, smart or casual, he would see her again with her hair flowing loose and falling like a curtain over one side of her face, just as it had all those years ago when she'd played Titania. Curiously, a little fizz of excitement spurted through her at the thought.

In the end she went for smart casual—black pumps, soft beige close-fitting velvet pants and a loose purple V-necked sweater. Her only jewellery was drop earrings and a tiny gold wrist-watch round her slender wrist.

'You'll do,' she told her reflection in the mirror, adding a touch more mascara to her long lashes and a final squirt of perfume down the V-neck of her sweater.

'Now why,' she asked herself as she searched through her wardrobe for a jacket, 'did I do that? I don't want to flirt with the man.'

Don't you? whispered a small voice deep inside her head.

She slung a black suede jacket round her shoulders and smiled. 'Well, just a little perhaps,' she murmured. 'After all, I can't hurt him, can I? He's woman-proof, so I won't be breaking the rules.'

'You look... Wow... Fantastic, I think the word is,' said Jeremy a few minutes later, when Veronica opened the door of the flat in answer to his ring. Not exactly a sophisticated, man-of-the-world compliment.

Good God, he hadn't meant to say that, but the words had seemed to leap out of their own accord. Tonight he had planned to be cool and professional. He wasn't on a date, he didn't have to throw compliments around. He was having a semi-professional meeting with an old friend—no, acquaintance would be more accurate. *She* had made it clear that that was how she thought of their teenage episode.

They were having dinner together to talk. Somehow he had to explain that Alec's interest in her scar was because she was one of his A and E team, and that in spite of his sometimes gruff manner Alec had a paternal approach to his younger colleagues.

As to his own interest in her, *that*, he reminded himself sharply, was purely professional. He had a mission, he must try to persuade her that he might be able to do something about the old scar tissue if only she would let him examine it...

'Jeremy, are you all right?' Veronica's ice-cool voice cut through his thoughts like a laser.

She was holding the door open wide, clearly inviting him in.

How long had he stood there? 'I'm fine, thanks—sorry,

I was thinking about a patient.' Well, there was an element of truth in that. He stepped into the narrow hall and followed her through to the spacious sitting room.

'Doctors tend to do that,' she said dryly. 'Sometimes at the most inopportune moments.'

Was she teasing? 'Sounds as if you know your doctors pretty well, and not only on duty.' His voice as dry as hers.

Was she playing the field? He found it hard to believe after what Alec had said and his own brief conversations with her over the last two days. No close friends, Alec had said, and he himself would have placed a bet on her being very choosy about her friends. But, then, what did either he or Alec know about her? She'd only been at Porthampton for a few weeks, and she was a damned good actress, as he had good cause to know. Perhaps her cool, regal look was all an act.

She had certainly dressed up for him tonight, or was this just normal gear for her? Her parents, as he remembered from those far-off school days, had been very comfortably off, so she certainly wasn't short of the odd pound or two.

Veronica didn't answer his half-question, but offered him a drink.

'Just a mineral water, please,' he replied. 'I restrict myself when driving to a glass of wine, which I'll have when we eat.'

'Will you have ice and lemon with it—the mineral water?'

'That will be a luxury I don't often worry about,' he replied.

She poured his drink and added ice and lemon, and poured a dry vermouth with ice and lemon for herself. A cool drink for a cool lady, he thought.

'Does that mean that you live by yourself?' she asked as she handed him the cut-glass tumbler filled with sparkling water, with ice cubes clanking invitingly.

'It does,' he said. 'I'm a bachelor by nature and intent and mean to stay that way.'

'Really, at thirty-two!' she exclaimed. 'How can you possibly be sure that's what you want—that you won't meet someone and fall for her?'

'Why is it,' he asked, 'that people, particularly women, can accept the concept of falling in love and forming a partnership at any age, yet not accept that some of us, men and women, prefer a solitary existence? And I emphasise *prefer* to live alone.'

Veronica took a large sip of her drink and swallowed it slowly. 'I don't know,' she said thoughtfully. 'Perhaps because man is a social animal and needs company.'

'Man as in mankind.'

'Of course.'

'And at twenty-eight, what plans have you made for getting married or forming a partnership, Veronica?' He emptied his glass and rolled it between his fingers. He watched, fascinated, as her hand immediately disappeared beneath the curtain of hair to cover her scar. The psychological effects of her scarring went very deep indeed. Trust Alec to have noticed how conscious she was of it.

She tossed off the last of her drink and said brightly, 'Oh well, it's different for me.' She looked at her tiny gold wrist-watch. 'Isn't it time we went if you've booked a table?' she said.

The restaurant attached to the Old Thatched Barn, tucked away in a fold in the south downs, was all that Jeremy had promised. It really was a barn, with great blackened beams and a thick thatch. The proprietors were big on fresh organic vegetables and meat and fish, the waiters well trained and invisible between courses. It must cost the earth to eat here, Veronica mused. Another indication of Jeremy's changed status.

Jeremy was obviously a regular and favoured customer. Their table was tucked away in an alcove beside a log fire, welcome on this chilly, showery March evening.

The herb pâté was full of flavour, spread on slivers of crunchy toast, and they both chose fresh trout lightly poached in white wine to follow. Jeremy recommended lamb chops with spring vegetables and tiny new potatoes, all locally produced, as their main course, and Veronica, complaining that she was already replete, gave in and was glad that she had. Everything was cooked to perfection and she wasn't surprised to see that the restaurant soon filled up and remained full for the rest of the evening.

'Let's have a lull,' Jeremy suggested, 'and enjoy our wine and talk while we consider our pudding. There's no rush.'

'But they seem to be awfully busy, they'll probably want our table later.'

Jeremy shook his head. 'No, this is ours for as long as we want it.' He was assured and confident.

Veronica said softly, 'What a long way you've come since Churchman's College.'

'You mean that the scholarship boy has acquired a patina of sophistication and gentlemanly behaviour since then?'

Veronica drew in a deep breath and the nostrils of her retroussé nose flared. 'No,' she said sharply,' 'I don't mean that. You always had a kind of sophistication even at school. No, it's more than that, it's as if you're at ease with yourself.' She shrugged. 'I can't really explain it.'

Jeremy held his glass up to the flickering light coming

from the fire, and it winked redly. 'Perhaps,' he said, 'it's because I'm doing the job that I always wanted to do and quite simply I've got job satisfaction. What about you, Veronica? Do you have job satisfaction?'

Veronica admired his well-shaped hands as they turned the wineglass, and the rounded and beautifully manicured nails—something else she'd never noticed about him when they'd been younger. He had the right sort of hands for the micro-surgery he performed, narrow, neat. He must, she thought, have a very gentle touch. No wonder he had such a fine reputation.

Belatedly she nodded in answer to his question. 'Oh, yes, I love my work. And being in A and E, although a lot of my day is taken up in administration, I can still do hands-on nursing, which is really my forte. In almost any other branch of nursing, I would have had to abandon hands-on care and concentrate on the admin side to make the grade—and that's not for me.'

Jeremy said softly. 'At thirteen you didn't seem a very likely candidate for nursing. Was it your accident that led you into it?'

'Yes, and I've never regretted it for an instant.' She put her elbows on the table and cupped her chin in her hands. The red-gold curtain of hair, shimmering like silk, swung down over the left side of her face. In her right ear, the amethyst drop earring swung and glowed.

Only her right eye, a misty grey, was visible to Jeremy as she inspected him gravely. 'When I had my accident, I nearly died, and as a lot of people do *in extremis*, I made all sorts of promises if I survived—not necessarily nursing, but to do something useful with my life.'

She smiled slightly. 'Ironically, I was backpacking round the Greek islands, trying to decide what career to go for, when I had my accident. I'd got some respectable

A-levels and had been accepted at a couple of universities. Banking appealed to me—my father was a merchant banker—and I liked computers and the idea of modelling or acting, but I couldn't make up my mind.'

'In other words, the world was your oyster,' murmured Jeremy, 'just as it had always been.' His eyes were midnight blue black pools and never left her face. 'So why, in the end, nursing?'

'After weeks in hospital I knew it had to be nursing. Nurses are the cement which holds everything else together—*if* they're dedicated to caring for people and not just academic nurses.' She frowned and made a dismissive gesture. 'But I mustn't get onto that subject—that and non-medical managerial staff are hobby-horses of mine.'

She picked up the discreet menu. 'I think that I'm ready to order pudding,' she said brightly. 'Is there anything that you can recommend?'

Jeremy brought himself down to earth with a thud. Her story had been fascinating and there was still so much that he wanted to know. It still seemed to him incredible that the spoilt girl he had known had turned into this calm, kind, self-contained woman.

'The apple and blackberry tart,' he said without hesitation. 'Made from their own fruit bottled last year and served with home-made custard.' He kissed two fingers. 'Out of this world.'

For a moment, Veronica thought, he looked the young, handsome man that he was, rather than the stern professor-like consultant that he sometimes portrayed. She chuckled, a low, rich chuckle that set his pulses racing. 'They should pay you for advertising,' she said.

His mouth quirked at one side. 'In a way they do,' he said, 'by always having a table available for me.' He lifted a hand to beckon a waiter and ordered their pudding.

His mobile buzzed just as she pushed her plate away a short time later. She sat back with a contented sigh. 'Beautiful,' she mouthed as Jeremy murmured into the instrument.

He answered in the affirmative a couple of times, then added, 'Be there in about half an hour.' He glanced across at Veronica. 'Sorry about that. A small child burned in a house fire. I'll have to go. The sooner I can see her, the sooner I might be able to do something for her, prevent too much long-term damage. If you want to stay and have coffee and a liqueur, please, do. I'll arrange for a taxi to take you back.'

Veronica stood up. 'I'd rather go with you. If there's been a fire, there are probably other people affected and A and E will be under pressure. There's been a football match tonight, too, and that always brings in a few bodies.'

Jeremy looked as if he was going to argue, but nodded. 'Right, let's be off, then.'

The small, badly burned girl had already been transferred to the burns unit next door to the plastic-surgery department on the second floor. Jeremy went straight up.

'Hate dealing with kids with burns,' he muttered, as he stepped into the lift. His lips compressed. 'Too heart-rending.'

So this self-contained man needed comforting. 'But at least you can do something really constructive for them,' said Veronica softly. 'Which is more than most of us can.'

A and E was much as she expected it to be. There was a noisy, belligerent group of young men in one corner of Reception, some of them still drinking from cans of lager. The main body of the room was almost full with tired, unhappy individuals trying to ignore the shouting and swearing.

Out of courtesy, Veronica went off to find night sister and offer her services, though as deputy nurse manager there was no need. Bella Courtney was in one of the cubicles, putting stitches into a cut forehead.

Veronica smiled at the patient and spoke to Bella through the gap between the curtains. 'Thought you might need a hand,' she said.

Bella's eyes lit up. 'A traditional angel of mercy,' she joked, 'though you need to cover your finery—looks as if you might have been out on the town.'

There was nothing to lose—it was as good a way as any to prevent the grapevine having a field day and blowing the evening out of proportion. 'I was having dinner with Jeremy Grant,' explained Veronica blandly, 'catching up on old times. We knew each other at school. I thought that I might be useful when he was called in on account of the burns victim.'

'And how,' said Bella. 'You must fill me in some time on what a night out with our Jeremy was like. Right now, if you could give me a hand with this lot…' she waved to indicate the cubicles and the waiting room '…I'd be grateful. The resus rooms are going strong, mostly smoke and burns victims, but the boss man himself and Dick Shepherd and most of my nursing staff are dealing with those. I'm on my own out here except for a couple of juniors and young Diana Ferguson as casualty officer. I must say that kid's got guts.'

'Yes she has,' replied Veronica. 'Give me a moment to change and I'm all yours.'

So Alec Masterson was here, though he probably didn't need to be. A consultant as senior as he didn't have to present himself for every emergency, but, then, he was like Jeremy, a workaholic, a dedicated doctor. A lonely man perhaps, who filled his days with work, though nobody seemed to know about his private life. Maybe he had a wife and a houseful of children.

It suddenly occurred to her as she changed into a spare uniform in her office that she and Jeremy hadn't discussed Alec at all during dinner, though that had been the object of the exercise.

A smile touched her lips as she made her way to the station to check who was to be seen next. It didn't really matter—it would give them an excuse to repeat tonight's successful dinner, tête-à-tête. That was, of course, if Jeremy had enjoyed the evening as much as she had... She hoped that he had.

'Oh, Veronica, how good to see you,' said Diana Ferguson, hurrying breathlessly from one of the cubicles. 'I'm trying to examine a small baby with what seems like a chest infection, only neither his mum nor the new student nurse seem to be able to keep him still. I can't get near him, he just shrieks and wriggles.'

The poor girl looked as if she might burst into tears at any moment. A familiar wave of anger washed over Veronica. It was the same old story. Admin, asked for another pair of hands, had sent an uninitiated junior who should only work under supervision, quite unsuitable for A and E, especially at night. Well, tomorrow she would have to do something about it, and if necessary rope in the boss himself to back her up. Alec Masterson was powerful enough to exercise some clout.

She squeezed Diana's arm. 'Come on,' she said cheerfully. 'I'm a whizz with fractious babies, we'll soon sort him out.'

'You're a whizz at everything,' said Diana, 'and you never lose your cool.'

If you could but see me raging inside, thought Veronica wryly as she followed the young doctor into the cubicle.

The cubicle looked a mess. The baby, about six months old, she guessed, was half-undressed, and baby clothes were strewn over the examination couch. A young girl of perhaps seventeen, presumably the mother, was bending over the tiny form making shushing sounds and was near to tears. And the young student nurse didn't look much better as she stood looking helplessly on.

Veronica took a deep breath. I'm surrounded by young and inexperienced staff, she thought, feeling suddenly old.

'Nurse.' She spoke quietly but firmly. 'Will you take Mum to get a drink while Doctor and I take care of...?'

'Sammy,' answered the student, looking relieved at the thought of escaping. She touched the young mother's arm. 'Come on, Tracy, let's go.'

'But I don't want to leave him,' Tracy sobbed as Sammy continued to bawl.

Veronica put an arm round her shoulders. 'Listen, Tracy, Sammy is picking up on your distress, which is making him cry even harder. He'll quieten down quicker if you're not here. Believe me, love, I've been looking after babies like Sammy for yonks and I know what I'm talking about, I really do.'

Tracy looked at her and frowned. 'Do you mean he can understand how worried I am?'

'He can, in his own way. You're the most important person in his life and he can sense that something is wrong.' While she was talking she scooped the baby up from the couch and pressed him firmly against her shoulder, keeping her hand on his back. The loud wailing diminished to a grizzle.

Tracy dropped a kiss on the top of Sammy's head. 'Mummy's going to have a drink. Be a good boy for

Nurse.' She blew her nose hard and allowed the student to lead her out of the cubicle.

Sammy had a severe chest infection and wheezed noisily whilst Diana examined him, but, soothed by Veronica's calm but firm handling, he had stopped crying.

Diana said enviously as she scribbled out a prescription for an infant antibiotic and painkiller, 'I wish I could handle children like that, but I don't seem to have much success with them.'

'It comes with practice,' replied Veronica, 'and it's important not to let them see that you're ruffled. They really do cue in quickly on our reactions.' She finished dressing Sammy and actually made him chuckle when she dropped a kiss on his nose and blew a raspberry. 'As a matter of fact,' she added, 'that applies to patients of any age.'

'That's the sort of thing they don't teach you in med school,' said Diana ruefully.

'That's true, and today's nurses aren't getting that sort of information either,' agreed Veronica. 'Once upon a time it was all part of our training. Now, do you want a word with Tracy before she goes?'

Diana nodded. 'I'd better. I want to explain about pushing fluids and so on, and tell her that she must call in her GP to see Sammy. She should have done that tonight instead of bringing him out, but apparently when she phoned she was told to keep him warm and take him to the surgery the following day.'

Veronica grimaced. 'Oh, one of those. If you don't mind me suggesting it, Diana, tell Tracy to inform him that she had to bring Sammy to A and E in the middle of the night, and that they advised that he comes to see her. Most of the local GPs like to keep in with the hospital, for they never know when they might need us.'

'Thanks for the advice. I'll do that.'

* * *

Veronica worked her way through the lager louts after Diana had given them cursory examinations, leaving the two younger nurses to deal with the other patients. To everyone's relief, she insisted that one of the security men stay in Reception to keep an eye on the noisy youths still waiting to be seen while she treated their mates one or two at a time in the cubicles. This restored some sort of order, and she was free to get on with stitching wounds and giving injections.

Dick Shepherd came through and joined her about half an hour after she'd begun working.

'I've done what I can with my second burns and smoke inhalation victim,' he explained. 'Jeremy Grant and the new registrar in the burns unit came down and looked at them, and they've been admitted upstairs. The boss is still at work on one of the firemen who is in one hell of a mess, but he just won't give up. My God, I just hope that if ever I'm in need of emergency surgery, Alec Masterson is around.'

'In the few weeks that I've been here, I've heard quite a few people making similar remarks.' Veronica replied as she finished fixing a support bandage round the hairy wrist of one of the football fans. 'There we are, Wayne, you're lucky not to have broken it. In future hit something softer than a six-foot-six all-in wrestler who favours the away team.' She examined his red, cracked and swollen knuckles. 'And when you get home, sit with your hand in a bag of frozen peas.'

Wayne nodded and growled sullenly, 'OK, will do.' He sidled out of the cubicle.

Dick Shepherd winked and said admiringly, 'And you've certainly got a way with you, Sister Lord.'

Veronica disposed of used instruments and dressings

and bobbed a curtsy. 'Well, thank you, kind sir. Now, have you come to help or just to chat?'

'The boss man sent me. I am here to serve. He's a bit concerned about young Diana, not that he put it like that, of course. I won't repeat his exact words.'

Veronica smiled. 'You'll find her in one of the cubicles across the way. The poor kid can do with some help, she's been working flat out.'

'So what's new?' said Dick, as with a mocking salute he left the cubicle.

With Dick's expert help and that of the two nurses who had been working with him in the resuscitation room, the number of patients waiting to be seen diminished rapidly and Veronica's help was no longer essential.

She reported off to Bella who was profuse in her thanks, and returned to her office to mull over the evening's events whilst she waited for Jeremy.

He arrived half an hour later, his face grim. He looked through rather than at Veronica.

'Let's go,' he said brusquely. 'Let's get out of this place and get some fresh air.'

Veronica nodded, remembering the look of anguish on his face as he'd got into the lift when they'd arrived three or four hours ago. 'Let's,' she said softly, putting a hand for a moment on his arm.

As the previous night, the car park was bathed in moonlight and the March air was now soft and balmy.

With the car windows down, they drove in silence up through the town toward the south downs and Heatherington House.

Jeremy stopped in the lane just before the drive to the house, but still didn't say anything. His dimly lit face gave nothing away as he stared down the hill at Porthampton, the busy sprawling city that straggled for miles along the coast. Even in the early hours of the morning there were plenty of lights shining. The major roads and the dockyard and the harbour, where several big liners were docked, were all well lit. The hospital was easy to identify. The windows of A and E and the theatres blazed with light, whilst the corridors and wards glowed dimly.

'What a ludicrous profession we're in,' he said suddenly, his voice harsh. 'Indifference, a never-ending workload, sometimes abusive patients...sometimes...' His voice trailed away.

Veronica felt as if her heart was being squeezed, this strong, hard man was in such a well of despair. She sat very still, trying to work out what she could do to help him, comfort him. 'Do you want to talk, Jeremy?'

He turned his head sharply and frowned, as if surprised to hear her voice. 'What? Oh, no, not now, some time maybe.' He switched on the engine and drove the few hundred yards to the front of Heatherington House, slid out of the driving seat and round to open the passenger door. He stood silently holding the door open.

Veronica undid her seat belt and swung her legs round, but didn't get out immediately. She looked up at his shadowed face. 'When you do want to talk, Jeremy,' she said softly. 'Remember that I'm a good listener.' She stood up and kissed his cheek. 'And thanks for an...interesting evening, the first bit especially.'

She didn't wait for a reply, but crossed to the front door, punched in her code and let herself in. She looked back before she closed the door. He was still standing there beside the car, a tall broad figure silhouetted against the moonlight.

Veronica waved and Jeremy raised his hand. 'Goodnight,' he called softly.

# CHAPTER FOUR

VERONICA fell asleep as soon as her head touched the pillow, but her sleep was troubled by nightmarish dreams, mostly of badly burned children. Little Sammy, the six-month-old infant with a chest infection, whom she had soothed and cuddled whilst Diana had examined him, suddenly metamorphosed in her dream into a baby with burns all over his little face. And she was working with Jeremy Grant in the plastic surgery theatre, not with Diana in A and E.

But Jeremy wasn't wearing theatre pyjamas or a mask, but his gorgeous satin and velvet Oberon costume as he bent over the operating table with a scalpel in his gloved hand—not surgical gloves, but bejewelled, cuffed, soft leather gauntlets. 'I'm about to about to pare away burnt skin,' he was saying in his rich, melodious voice to the nurses and technicians milling around. 'It's a priority before one starts repairing the damaged areas.'

And Veronica, standing opposite him on the other side of the operating table where an assistant surgeon should have been, knew that something was wrong, but couldn't speak or move. Infection, she wanted to scream out. What about infection? You should be operating in a sterile field. She could feel sweat running down between her breasts and down her spine to the crease of her buttocks, but was still rooted to the spot.

Then suddenly Jeremy was straightening up, stretching his arms and stepping back from the table. 'There, I think that'll do. This little chap's going to grow up to be a handsome young lady-killer.'

Everyone looked down at Sammy, who was wide awake and beaming with not a mark on his face, a chubby little boy with a scar-free future before him.

Veronica fought her way up from under her duvet and reached her hand out to the bedside cabinet for her mobile, which was buzzing insistently. The remnants of her dream hung over her, her heart was hammering uncomfortably and she had to clear her throat before answering, 'Veronica Lord.'

The senior receptionist's voice whispered quickly in a conspiratorial manner. 'It's Rebecca… Look, I know that you're not on till later and were up half the night, Veronica, and I'm sorry to worry you, but Frank's rung in sick—God knows when he's ever well—and things are a bit chaotic down here. Several cases of food poisoning that's thought to be salmonella have been reported on one of the liners that docked last night, and we're on the receiving line for those who can't be nursed on board. The first batch have just arrived to be processed to the wards, but—'

'I'm on my way.' Veronica slammed the receiver down and fumed over Frank Smithers as she had the speediest shower ever and automatically slapped on her disguising make-up. He'd had so many days off since she'd arrived that she felt that she hardly knew him.

'Frank's always conspicuous by his absence,' somebody had said, and though she had thought this an exaggeration she had learned that it was only too true. Why he hadn't taken early retirement nobody seemed to know, and she hadn't pushed, feeling that as his deputy it would have smacked of disloyalty.

But today she felt distinctly irritated by his apparent

lack of interest in the department. Another pair of experienced hands and executive know-how would have been invaluable. Instead of which she was finding herself, yet again, shouldering full responsibility. Her mind began grappling with the problems ahead.

The incoming patients would have to be segregated from the others in Reception and warded where they could have separate toilet facilities to prevent the spread of infection. Basic hygiene was the first line of defence in food-poisoning cases, and not widely enough publicised.

Alec was coming out of his office as Veronica came out of hers.

'Alerted by Rebecca, no doubt,' he said, his lip curling sardonically. 'You shouldn't be here till ten, and after the stint you put in last night...' He shrugged. 'But we're grateful. Let's say that it's not gone unnoticed and when Frank *does* retire, well...

'Now, about this outbreak. We're not yet sure if this is salmonella or some other bacterial infection, but I'm playing it safe. All the usual symptoms are there—diarrhoea, vomiting, headache. We've only admitted half a dozen so far, two children and four elderly people. I'm going to look at them now, but I dare say they're all dehydrated. So it's fluids plus and IV lines in as necessary. At the moment they're in the side corridor, which has been put out of bounds to other patients, with a security guard to endorse it.'

'Right. I'll arrange for a senior staff nurse to look after them till they're warded. They're going to need barrier nursing till we know what the bug is that's affecting them. I doubt there'll be enough room on the medical wards or acute nursing, so where will they go?'

'I've persuaded the upstairs people...' Alec jerked his

thumb upwards, indicating the admin offices '...to reopen the ward they closed last week and, by fair means or foul, to get enough nurses in to staff it, at whatever cost. The horrific picture I painted of the press swarming all over the place and questions being asked in the House if this outbreak wasn't contained seems to have done the trick.'

He produced one of his tight smiles.

'Oh, that's brilliant,' Veronica said. 'We could do with an overspill unit permanently to prevent patients clogging up the corridors whilst they're waiting to be warded.'

Alec stopped abruptly and laid a hand on her arm to hold her back. 'On our budget? You've got to be joking, Veronica,' he said.

He'd called her Veronica! This cold, detached man, whom she suspected wasn't really cold and detached, had called her by her first name. Stunned for a moment, she continued to stand still as he moved off down the corridor, then she had to move smartly to catch up with him.

The pace didn't stop all day. Nine more passengers from the cruise ship were admitted, and sent straight up to the overspill ward. Veronica sent a male nurse to help Janice and phoned Personnel for a domestic helper to assist with the clearing up.

She cut off their usual excuses, borrowing Alec's line, by saying sharply, 'Well, if you want the world and his wife to know that a possibly infectious ward isn't being properly cleaned and disinfected...' She left the idea floating in the air and put down the phone.

A quarter of an hour later a cleaner appeared, a cheerful, middle-aged woman. She seemed undismayed by a ward full of people being sick. 'I'm Pat,' she announced. 'Where do you want me to start, Sister?'

Veronica gave her a welcoming smile. 'You're a sight

for sore eyes,' she told her. 'Were you told that these patients are possibly infectious and you'll have to wear a special overall while you are working here? And, of course, personal standards of hygiene must be observed and you must wash your hands after handling dirty linen or finishing a cleaning job, even though you're wearing rubber gloves.'

'They didn't tell me direct, but everyone knows that there's something up and that's why this ward's been re-opened. But it don't worry me, Sister. I've brought up six kids and know all about dirty beds and clearing up sick and keeping everywhere clean.'

'Thank the Lord for sending me someone mature and sensible,' Veronica muttered, after she'd kitted Pat out and sent her in the direction of the sluice room.

With one exception, the latest admissions were all children or elderly. The exception was a young woman eighteen weeks pregnant, escorted by an almost hysterical young husband making all sorts of impossible demands.

The registrar from Obstetrics and Maternity was called in to examine her, and it was decided to move her to a side ward in that department. 'So that we can keep an eye on her and the baby,' he explained to the anxious husband, who, somewhat reassured, went with his wife to give her what comfort he could.

'Young love,' exclaimed Janice, wryly, rolling her eyes at Veronica and offering a vomit bowl and a supporting arm to a heaving patient.

After she had finished vomiting, the elderly woman lay back against her pillows which Janice had plumped up and turned over to the cool side. She gratefully gulped the iced water that Janice held to her lips.

'Thank you, Nurse. You are good,' she said. 'They're on their honeymoon, you know, that young couple, and so happy until this happened. Will the baby be all right, do you think? She won't have a miscarriage, will she, young Sandra?' She looked from Veronica to Janice. Then, before either of them could answer, she gasped. 'Oh, dear, I need the bedpan again, please.'

Back in A and E proper after the welcome arrival of two nurses produced by Personnel, Veronica was astonished to find Jeremy waiting for her in her office.

'Oh!' she exclaimed, pausing in the doorway. It was a pleasure, she realised, to see him studying the duty chart, looking sartorially correct in an expensive dark suit, the uniform of all the top consultants even in these enlightened days. He had broken her nightmarish dream.

He swung round from the chart and took a step toward her. 'Veronica! I hope you don't mind. The receptionist said it would be OK if I waited for you in here,' he explained.

As if as a consultant he needed anyone's permission to use her office, Veronica thought wryly, but it was a nice gesture and much appreciated.

His face, she thought, looked animated and there was a slight flush on his lightly tanned cheeks. With his back half to the window, she couldn't see if his dark eyes reflected his animation.

She said. 'You and Alec have a penchant for my duty chart, though I can't think why.' She waved him to a chair but he perched on the corner of her desk as she sat down behind it.

'I can't speak for Alec,' he said, 'but I wanted to check when you were off duty, though I guess that your hours, like mine, are elastic.'

'True.' Veronica nodded. 'And why are you interested in my off-duty time?' Silly, vacuous comment. She wished she hadn't made it. It had to be because he wanted to ask her out again and he must know that she would have guessed that.

'I thought that we might go out to dinner again to make up for last night's...disaster?' Jeremy was looking at her steadily.

'It wasn't all a disaster,' she said. 'The meal was perfect, but I'm so sorry that it had to end the way it did.' She pictured him getting into the lift last night, his face pale, his words bitter. 'And how is your poor little girl with burns?' she added.

'Hanging in there. The burns unit people are great and we were able to do minimum holding repairs together, without damaging her further, leaving a clean field to work in when she's fit enough for more surgery. She's a fighter, I think, little as she is, and I have hopes of being able to prevent any serious scarring.'

Veronica's hand went up to her face as it always did when she was reminded of her scar and as Jeremy had guessed that it would. Tentatively he reached out and stroked her hand, and she smiled slightly, appreciating the gesture.

'Oh, I'm so glad,' she said, and was almost tempted to tell him of her dream, but didn't.

At his brief touch, her usual cool seemed to have completely deserted her, though she was at a loss to know why. Not true! Who are you kidding? she asked herself scathingly. Of course you know why. It's because Jeremy is sitting only a few feet away, swinging one long leg and smelling of a mixture of pine and antiseptic soap.

Her breathing seemed to have gone haywire and she tried hard to get it under control. She fiddled with some papers and picked up a pen.

Jeremy leaned across the desk and with two fingers

tilted up her chin and looked down into her upturned face. 'You're a lovely woman, Veronica,' he murmured. He bent nearer and seemingly of their own volition her lips parted, waiting for his kiss. But his mouth never met hers. His lips instead brushed across her scar, tracking it from above her eyebrow to her cheekbone. 'I may be able to do something about this,' he said softly, 'if you'll let me.'

Veronica sat very still and felt her cheeks go pale. She gripped the arms of her chair. Whatever made me think that he's attracted to me personally? His work is paramount. My scar's a challenge and that's all that interests him. He and Alec Masterson are two of a kind. The thoughts milled around in her brain as she tried to make some sort of sense of them.

Jeremy slid off the edge of the desk and faced her, spreading his hands on its full width. 'I'm not promising you anything, I can't, but I'm very willing to try if you'll let me.'

Her voice came back to her at last, and with a supreme effort she pitched it low and steady. 'It's very kind of you, Jeremy, but I don't need help now. If someone like you or Alec had been around when my accident happened, yes. But you weren't. There was only a rather pompous little Greek village doctor who stitched me up, and that was that. And I had other injuries that were more important. I've had ten years to come to terms with it, and I have.'

She picked up the phone. 'Look, I must make this call and then do a round outside.'

Jeremy straightened up slowly.

'So, it wasn't a car accident that caused your injury?'

'No! I was caught up in an earthquake on a small Greek island. Why did you assume that it was a car accident?'

He waved the question away. 'Most accidents are. And

this happened ten years ago?' There was a question in his voice.

'Yes, in June. Now, I really must get on, Jeremy.'

*June ten years ago!* He'd been there, touring the islands, ten years ago, and he'd been involved in an earthquake. It couldn't be the same one, no way. There were dozens of Greek islands, dozens of minor earthquakes. His mind gabbled the facts. But there'd been a girl, unrecognisable because of her injuries. He'd wanted to help, but the local doctor—a pompous little man—had sent him away, had insisted that he should go.

Jeremy went deathly cold. He felt the blood drain from his face and a band of iron tighten round his heart. *His earthquake had been Veronica's earthquake!* There were too many coincidences that couldn't be ignored, right down to the 'pompous little doctor', whom he'd allowed to dismiss him.

He almost groaned out aloud. If only he'd stayed he might have prevented...

He said, his usually melodious voice rough, brusque, 'I'll take you out for supper tonight, after you come off duty at ten. I'll meet you in the car park at ten-fifteen.'

Veronica raised her eyebrows and stared at him. What had brought on that tone of voice? He looked rather pale, his eyes dark and filled with pain. 'Are you all right, Jeremy?'

'I'm fine. So how about supper—please, say yes?'

She shook her head. She didn't think that she could contemplate an evening with him after making a fool of herself, thinking that he was going to kiss her, even though he probably hadn't noticed her parted lips.

'No, thanks. All I'll want to do then is to bath and crash out and not even bother to change out of uniform.'

'Let's go to the all-night caff round the corner for fish

and chips and strong tea. Hospital uniform is practically *de rigueur* there, it's almost an overflow for the canteen. Please, Veronica, I *must* talk to you...it's imperative.'

On the point of refusing again, the pleading in his voice and manner made her think twice. She nodded. 'All right, but a quick supper and then home.'

'Fair enough.' He sounded relieved. He moved to the door and paused. 'You know, whoever said that the Lord moves in mysterious ways His wonders to perform was dead right. We're not often given a chance to put right a wrong.' He raised his hand and moved into the corridor, closing her door softly behind him.

She wouldn't let herself dwell on what he had meant by that. It was too complicated and she had a stack of work to do.

His hands in trouser pockets, head and shoulders hunched, eyes focused on the floor, Jeremy walked slowly along the corridor. His brain whirling, thick with images and memories from the past, he literally bumped into Alec.

They apologised to each other.

'Looking for me?' Alec asked.

Jeremy was tempted to say yes and avoid any questions about Veronica, but his innate honesty wouldn't let him and he couldn't prevaricate with Alec of all people...at least, not unless he absolutely had to.

'No, I've been having a chat with Veronica.'

'Good. Are you making any progress with her? Do you think that she'll let you do anything about her scar?'

'Too soon to say Alec. Perhaps having dinner with her last night would have borne fruit but, of course, that was cut short by the emergency call. And there was no opportunity later when we eventually got away. But we're going to have supper together when she comes off duty tonight, although she'll be tired and we have a lot to talk about, catching up on old times.'

'Yes, of course you have.' Alec placed a hand on Jeremy's arm. 'Has something happened that has stirred things up? Unhappy memories perhaps?' he asked. 'You look shattered.'

*Shattered!* Yes, he was certainly that. If you only knew how the past has come home to haunt me, he thought. For a moment he was tempted to confide in Alec, tell him of his fears that he had been involved in the earthquake that had scarred Veronica—acknowledge that he might, just *might* have prevented it happening, if only he hadn't walked away…

But he was reluctant to tell Alec at this moment. What would his reaction be to Jeremy's suggestion that he might have prevented the worst happening to Veronica, had he shown a spark of courage? His self-esteem was so low that he couldn't bear to risk Alec's condemnation.

Alec was peering at him closely. 'What's wrong, Jeremy? You look a bit grey round the gills. Would it help to talk about it?'

Jeremy shook his head. 'A lot on my mind,' Jeremy replied. 'Must get back—a tricky piece of surgery this afternoon.'

A work problem. This was something that Alec understood and respected, and if there was something more personal on his friend's mind, he would learn more of that when Jeremy was good and ready to divulge it. For the moment, he was prepared to accept that what was bothering Jeremy most was the operation ahead of him.

He nodded. 'May the gods go with you,' he said, which was the good-will mantra that they exchanged when either of them were facing a complex medical problem.

'Thanks.' Jeremy marched away down the corridor toward the bank of lifts.

Once in the crowded lift, he concentrated on emptying his mind of everything except the coming operation. For although he had mentioned it to distract Alec, he *did* have a difficult piece of surgery to perform. Now was not the time to dwell on Veronica, her scar or her accident, or his part in it.

By the time he reached his floor with its own plastic surgery theatre, he was able to bring all his concentration to bear on the young woman, aged twenty-four, he was to operate on. He went straight to the viewing room to look at the blown-up X-rays of Marie Stone's misaligned jaw, a misalignment so bad that she hadn't been able to eat normally for months.

He made notes and sketches, as he always did, as he viewed the X-rays. Little arrows indicated the direction he would have to move the upper jaw, and stars indicated where he would have to remove or put tucks into loose folds of skin. It would be a longish op, six, seven hours, and there would be more to follow. It was due to start at twelve-thirty. He looked at his watch—it was coming up to twelve.

Marie would have already had her pre-med and be drowsy, but he would pop in and see her before he went through to scrub up.

Marie was pathetically pleased to see him, although she was too drowsy to speak and in any case talking, because of the overhanging upper jaw, made speech almost impossible. But she squeezed Jeremy's hand and mumbled something that sounded like, 'Thank you.'

Jeremy nodded and squeezed her hand in return, and went off to get gowned and scrubbed up.

* * *

A and E were busy all the afternoon, but it was the usual cut and thrust of emergencies. A coronary that, through the magnificent efforts of the crash team, avoided becoming a death statistic. A messy attempt at suicide by a young man who had tried to cut his wrists and who needed psychological rather than physical help. Veronica stayed with him for a while, listening to him rambling on about being lonely yet refusing to go back home to what appeared loving parents.

A child was brought in who was thought to have swallowed some sleeping tablets belonging to her mother. But neither a scan nor a thorough physical and question-and-answer examination revealed anything. A stomach wash-out was considered, but Dick Shepherd opted to dismiss this unpleasant treatment if it could be avoided and it was decided to send the little girl up to the children's ward for an overnight stay and observation.

Late in the afternoon an elderly lady, who had fallen in the garden and fractured her femur, was brought in by the paramedics, called by a neighbour who had seen her lying on the ground from a bedroom window.

'Don't know how long she'd been lying in the garden,' explained one of the ambulance crew, 'but she was suffering from a degree of hypothermia when we got to her and she's only just warming up.'

Veronica and a junior nurse on work selection carefully undressed the elderly lady, Mrs Muriel Cook. 'Call me Mirry, dear,' she said drowsily, when the junior was filling in her admission form.

'OK,' said the junior cheerfully. 'And how old are you, Mirry?'

Veronica, who made a habit of occasionally accompanying students on work experience to assess how they were doing, hid a smile at the ease with which the young nurse complied with Mrs Cook's suggestion without sounding too cheeky. She'd make a good A and E nurse, Veronica decided, and made a mental note to keep a special eye on her.

The age barrier didn't seem to bother her in the least and until given permission, she had followed Veronica's lead and addressed the patient as Mrs Cook.

It was another of Alec Masterson's rules that elderly patients were always addressed formally unless they requested otherwise.

'It's a small courtesy amongst all the indignities that they often have to suffer in hospital,' he said.

There were no more cases of food poisoning admitted. Laboratory results confirmed the outbreak as salmonella, but a manager, speaking on behalf of the hospital to the inevitable band of journalists waiting to pounce, was able to say, as if it had been all his doing, that it had been contained because of the strict precautions taken—no expense spared.

Veronica and one of the registrars, watching the early evening news on the television in the staff room, both snorted derisively. 'You'd think,' said Noella Davis, a newly appointed registrar, 'that he would throw a bit of credit Alec Masterson's way. If he hadn't suggested—'

'You've got to be joking,' replied Veronica. 'And I suppose at the end of the day it's more important that the hospital comes up smelling of roses, rather than any individual.'

Toward the end of the evening things began to calm down and Veronica closeted herself in her office to catch up on paperwork. And she wanted to unwind enough to think through the extraordinary conversation she'd had with

Jeremy. What *had* he meant by being given a second chance?

'The mind boggles,' she said out loud, and found that she was looking forward to that night's supper with a mixture of pleasure and trepidation.

Jeremy was waiting for her in the car park when she came off duty at twenty past ten. One look at his face in the brilliant lighting of the car park told her that he was drained, exhausted.

'You've had a bad day,' she said quietly, laying a hand on his sleeve. 'Let's shelve supper, we can do it some other time. You need to get home to bed.'

He shook his head. 'Nope, fish and chips and gallons of sweet tea are just what the doctor ordered.'

Veronica recognised the symptoms. Exhausted he might be, but he wasn't ready to turn off the adrenaline and the endorphins were still circulating like mad. He needed time to wind down.

The café was almost full even at this time of night. There were lorry drivers and a fair sprinkling of hospital staff who acknowledged them with a nod. They found a table in the window, which was all steamed up with hot breath and hot food, and seated themselves gratefully.

A few minutes later a middle-aged woman, looking, Veronica thought, as exhausted as they were, came to take their order. She wavered a smile at Jeremy. 'Another late night, Mr Grant?' she asked sympathetically.

Jeremy gave her a relaxed grin. 'You and me both, Jean,' he said. He turned toward Veronica. 'I don't know if you've met Sister Lord, she's a colleague.'

'I know,' replied Jean. 'We've met, but not here. I was in Casualty about three weeks ago. Burnt my arm on the tea urn and you slapped on a bag of ice and then put a special dressing on it which worked like magic on the pain. It's all healed up now thanks to you.'

'Not me.' Veronica laughed. 'It was the ice and the dressing that did it.'

'Oh, well, whatever, I'm grateful. Now, what can I tempt you with?'

Jeremy ordered the fish and chips that he'd promised Veronica and a large pot of tea. Jean brought the tea almost at once and a bowl of sugar.

She winked at Jeremy. 'Know you'd rather have this than open dozens of those fiddly little packets,' she said, and then, without being asked, she poured tea into the two breakfast-sized mugs. 'Enjoy,' she said, and disappeared toward the kitchen.

Veronica watched Jeremy shovel several spoonfuls of sugar into his tea. 'What's with this VIP treatment you seem to get at all the local eating establishments?' she queried.

He took a cautious sip of the scalding liquid and sighed with pleasure. 'Best reviver of them all, the cup that cheers without inebriating.' He took another sip. 'Not that I'm against a good malt from time to time.'

Veronica raised an eyebrow. 'You're prevaricating, Jeremy.'

He looked embarrassed. 'Some patients are extremely grateful for whatever's done for them,' he said. 'I did some work on Jean's granddaughter a while back—she had a cleft palate and a harelip. I'll have to do a bit more work on it at a later date, but it came out pretty well and...' He spread his nice competent hands. 'And well, Jean appreciated what I did.'

Jeremy was full of surprises, thought Veronica, almost two different men—the doctor who could occasionally be cold and authoritative, and the almost shy gentle man she was seeing before her now. But which one was the real Jeremy Grant?

She felt so relaxed in the warm, stuffy atmosphere that she might have asked him had their steaming plates of fish and chips not arrived at that moment, together with a mound of bread and butter.

'*Bon appetit*,' he said, lifting his huge mug in salute. 'Get stuck in, a high carbohydrate meal is exactly what we need right now. And when we've finished, we'll either talk or I'll take you home and you can sleep the sleep of the angels.'

# CHAPTER FIVE

THE fish and chips and thick bread and butter were delicious, the tea as it should be, strong and reviving.

Veronica swallowed a final mouthful of bread and butter and glanced across at Jeremy. He had finished eating and seemed absorbed in the contents of his mug. He was looking rather better than he had in the car park. The drained look had almost gone, but his expression when he raised his head and stared silently at her was unreadable. She picked up her mug, took a sip of tea and tried to think of how she might break the silence.

The silence hadn't mattered when they'd been eating, they'd both been hungry and had needed their food, but now it was taut and uneasy and full of things unsaid, and the reason for them being here in this steamy little café, suddenly loomed large. He wanted to talk, he'd said. No, he'd been more forceful than that, not wanted—*needed.* It was a must and it was somehow tied up with this business of the Lord working in mysterious ways.

It was such a strange expression for Jeremy to use, she mused. She hadn't put him down as a religious man, he was a dedicated man of science. Not that that necessarily precluded him from believing in God, but… But nothing! She didn't know this man, this adult Jeremy Grant, she was jumping to conclusions.

She drank the last of her cooling tea but continued to hold the empty mug—it gave her something to do with her hands.

Looking over the rim, she said softly, 'Jeremy, you wanted to talk, so let's talk.'

He said curtly. 'Sorry, I can't, not here.'

'But you suggested here,' Veronica argued.

'I thought it would be neutral enough, but it's not—there are too many white coats.' He nodded toward a group of young doctors and nurses who had just sat down at a table. He stood up abruptly. 'Let's go, to my place or yours!'

The classic remark didn't have any overtones as it might have done had they been lovers: he simply wanted to know what would suit her best. Veronica stood up, too. She thought about suggesting that they put off the talk until tomorrow, but one look at his face told her that he wouldn't agree. And in any case she wasn't at all sure that she could contain her curiosity any longer.

'Mine,' she said. 'Yours is buried somewhere in the country, isn't it?'

Jeremy nodded but didn't offer any information. She made her way to the door while he paid for their supper.

They walked in silence the short distance back to the hospital and each made for their own car. Jeremy swept out through the main gates just in front of her and was waiting by the front door of Heatherington House when she drew up minutes after him.

Now that they were there Veronica felt distinctly nervous and a shiver of anticipation tingled through her as she punched in the code and then inserted her key.

'Cold?' he asked, but she guessed that he knew the answer and she didn't bother to confirm or deny it.

As soon as they got into the flat she put on coffee to percolate. 'After all that tea,' she explained vaguely over her shoulder from the kitchen. 'And I thought that a glass of wine wouldn't come amiss. After all it'll be a while yet before you have to drive and it shouldn't make much impact on top of that huge supper…'

He was prowling round the sitting room, scowling with concentration. Veronica stopped him in mid-prowl and thrust a bottle of red wine and an opener into his hands. 'Please,' she said when he stared at it as if it were something unmentionable. But he opened it with a few neat turns of the corkscrew and handed it back to her.

'Are you going to be long,' he muttered irritably, 'manufacturing reasons for not sitting down before I lose my nerve?'

'I didn't think that you had nerves,' she said before she could stop herself.

'Really,' he snorted.

She shook her head, took glasses from a small cupboard, poured out the wine and sat down in one of the cane chairs flanking the fireplace. The fireplace was filled with an urn full of fragrant spring flowers. Veronica sniffed gratefully: flowers were simple and straightforward, producing no awkward surprises.

Jeremy sat down in the opposite chair. His high forehead was scored with horizontal lines and two deep vertical lines pulled his arched brows together above his nose. 'What do you think the chances are,' he asked, 'of two people who once knew each other meeting up in unlikely circumstances and neither recognising the other, and then meeting up again in more conventional circumstances years later?' He leaned forward, his elbows on knees, and his dark eyes, very intense, caught and held hers. A shiver went down her spine.

Veronica felt herself go cold. 'You're talking about us,' she whispered, 'aren't you?'

He nodded, still keeping eye contact.

'But how could we meet and not recognise each other?

I don't understand. And where were these unusual circumstances?' She took a great gulp of wine and almost choked.

'In Greece, in the middle of an earthquake,' he said, his voice flat. 'I was touring the Greek islands at the same time as you were, ten years ago. I helped pull you out of a crevice that had opened up...'

He paused and Veronica stared at him unable to speak.

'You were hanging onto a small boy with what little strength you had. Your face was streaked with blood and dirt, and your lovely hair was smothered in a thick layer of grey dust. Had I seen your hair...'

He reached across the small space between them and touched her hair with one hand, smoothing back a strand or two that had escaped from the restraining combs.

Veronica heard him saying something through the clamouring that was going on inside her head. Her own hand shaking, she gripped his and pulled it away from her face. She was conscious of two spots of heat on her cheekbones and she felt sick with a growing rage. '*You were there*,' she whispered incredulously, ferociously, '*and you walked away from me*?'

Jeremy flinched at the expression in her steel grey eyes. He heaved in a deep breath and said evenly, 'But I didn't know it was you, Veronica, that's what I am trying to explain. Had I known, nothing, or no one, would have persuaded me to abandon you.'

The contempt he read in her face made him feel incredibly small and worthless.

'But you abandoned the poor girl you'd helped to rescue to that pompous, ignorant little doctor. *Not* a very caring attitude to take, was it?' she ground out through clenched teeth.

Jeremy stood up, gathering the remnants of his strength

around him. He didn't blame her for looking at him the way she was, but he had to make her understand what it had been like on that day. The noise, the dust, the stifling heat, the foreign voices, his reluctance to be pushy as he'd only just qualified—and above all, his belief that the girl was from the village and should be treated by her own doctor.

How could he make this woman who had reappeared in his life understand? He went to the window and opened it and stared out at the starry night sky, seeking inspiration. He wasn't looking for excuses, he didn't have any, but somehow he had to convince her that he hadn't just walked away, he'd been driven away by the local doctor, a man twice his age, with twice his experience and in his own territory.

He became aware of Veronica, sitting tensely, shocked, full of bitterness and anger, hardly able to comprehend what he'd told her. But he had to defend himself against her accusation of being uncaring.

He turned round slowly, drained his glass and indicated the bottle standing on the table. 'May I?'

She stared at him for a moment, then nodded. 'Do, and top mine up, too, please, I've a feeling that I'm going to need it.'

Their glasses full, he sat down again in the chair opposite hers. 'I'm not and never was an uncaring doctor, Veronica. You do me an injustice if you think otherwise. Believe me, I regret what happened that day, wish that I could rewrite the script, but I can't. I was twenty-two, just qualified and in a foreign country with their own rules and regulations.'

He sipped his wine. 'You were almost unconscious and I assumed that you were a local girl who would be better off with people whom she knew. There was nothing callous about my decision to leave. I think that you should accept that. And Dr *Pompous*, for want of a better name, ordered me away.'

Veronica looked up at the smooth, handsome face set in grim lines. It was a cool, dispassionate plea for her understanding rather than her forgiveness.

And then he turned that thought on its head, by saying in a low, husky voice, 'Can you forgive me, Veronica?' He leaned forward until his midnight blue eyes were only a few inches from hers of steely grey.

Now he was appealing to her heart rather than her head. Could she forgive him? It was hard to believe that he hadn't recognised her, she was sure that she would have recognised him under similar circumstances. No, that's not right, she was accusing him of being a liar, and angry as she was she knew that he was no liar.

Did he understand the hurt that she was suffering? Didn't he realise that the fact that he had been there all those years ago made everything that much worse? The knowledge that had he stayed with her, *this*—she touched her scar—might have been avoided. She didn't want logical reasoning, she wanted...

He must have read her mind, for suddenly he was there in front of her, drawing her to her feet, removing her glass from stiff fingers and pulling her into his arms in one smooth movement. For a moment she stood still, letting her body relax against his, abandoning herself to the wave of pleasure that washed over her.

For the first time in a long while she felt utterly safe and secure. She could have stayed in his arms for ever.

Then her practical, common-sense self took over, and she murmured breathlessly into his shirtfront. 'Jeremy, please, let me go. I don't want this.'

He nuzzled the top of her head and slowly loosened his arms, allowing her to draw away from him.

He said with husky tenderness, 'I wish to God that you did, my love. But I'm used to waiting for what I want to happen. I've spent a lifetime perfecting patience. It's a positive requirement in my job and it certainly was in my teenage years. Waiting, hoping for my wretched acne to disappear, spending most of my pocket money on the latest cure… Remember, Veronica?'

Of course she remembered—it was a joke amongst her set. How cruel could you get? She missed the feel of Jeremy's arms supporting her, and sat down with a slight bump.

Remorse flooded through her as it hit her forcefully that instead of expecting him to feel guilty for having abandoned her in Greece it was she who should feel guilty for the unhappiness she'd caused him when they'd both still been at school.

'But I didn't mean to hurt you,' she whispered, as if he knew what she was thinking. 'I was young and silly and incredibly selfish.'

Evidently he did know what she was thinking, for he said softly, 'Exactly. When we're young we say and do stupid, selfish things—that was the point I was making. I opted out of insisting that I stay to help on the day of the earthquake, for the reasons I've already given. I would gladly have stayed had I been needed, but I wasn't so I went back to the boat and got on with my holiday. Not very noble motives, but there you go.'

Veronica felt faintly sick as they sat looking at each other, separated by a yard or so. He could easily have reached out and touched her or taken her into his arms again, but he didn't. Not that she was sure she wanted him to. In fact, she wasn't sure of anything at all. He was waiting for her to say or do something—but what?

Her heart was pumping away like mad, as if it might jump out of her chest wall at any moment, and she was finding breathing difficult. She was so conscious of him. He seemed to be emanating wave after wave of masculine strength across the small space between them. Why on earth was he having this effect on her when a few minutes ago she could have murdered him?

They both stood up and she half reached out to touch him, but drew back. After an interminable silence, she said, 'I'm lost. Where do we go from here, Jeremy?'

She could find no help in his dark eyes—they looked like fathomless pools, and his aquiline nose more than usually daunting.

'I rather think—' his voice was gruff but gentle '—that'll be up to you, Veronica. I'll go along with whatever you want. But you've got a while to think about it. I shall be away at a conference for a few days from tomorrow.'

He sketched a salute, strode toward the door and let himself out while she stood rooted to the spot. She heard his footsteps fade away along the hall—and then, woodenly, she moved to the window and watched him drive away in the moonlight.

Why hadn't he warned her that he was going away, that he was abandoning her yet again, just when she needed him and there was so much that they had to say to each other?

Tonight's revelations had given a whole new meaning to their briefly renewed relationship, but whether for better or for worse, she couldn't figure out.

After a sleepless night, Veronica went to work the next morning with a raging headache.

'Heavens, you look dreadful,' Janice greeted her.

'Thanks for those few kind words.' Veronica's voice was heavy with sarcasm. 'And you look on top of the world in spite of being knee deep in—'

Janice held up her hands in mock horror. 'Don't say it. I'm just on my way up to check on how my poor cruise victims are doing. The boss thought that several of them might be discharged today if all goes well, so keep your fingers crossed for me.'

Veronica held up crossed fingers. 'Will do, we need you back down here.' She continued on her way to Reception to do a rough head count and ran into Alec Masterson striding down the corridor toward her.

He looked more than usually grim. 'That's all I need,' Veronica muttered, *sotto voce*. 'The boss in a bad temper.'

She pinned a smile on her face and wished him good morning as they got closer.

He stopped in front of her. 'Sister...Veronica...did you know that Jeremy was going to be away for several days?'

His abruptness was par for the course, but she was surprised by his question and his use again of her first name. Surely if anyone would know that Jeremy was to be away, it would be Alec. After all, he and Jeremy were friends as well as colleagues. So if Jeremy hadn't told him, perhaps it was because he didn't want him to know. No, that didn't make sense. Why be secretive about a medical conference?

It dawned on her that maybe the reason he hadn't told Alec, or herself till last night, was because he hadn't known himself till late yesterday that he would be going.

Alec was frowning heavily, his straight brows beetling together. 'Well, did you know that he was going away?'

'He told me late last night that he was going to a conference, but he didn't say where.'

Alec looked relieved. 'York,' he said crisply, 'but he was going to give that a miss, thought it might be on the dull side since the speaker he particularly wanted to hear wasn't going to be present.' He seemed lost in thought for a moment.

'Perhaps,' Veronica suggested, 'something happened at the last minute to make him change his mind.'

'Evidently,' he replied. He looked up and down the empty corridor, dropped his voice and said quietly, 'Veronica, dine with me tonight...please.' The 'please' sounded like an afterthought.

She noticed the colour of his eyes for the first time, though they had often worked opposite each other and she had seen them express concern and anger. But their colour hadn't registered—now she saw that they were brown.

To say that she was surprised didn't begin to explain how she was feeling. Had her boss really invited her out? Apparently, but why?

'Well?' Alec's clipped tones cut through her thoughts.

'It's kind of you...Alec,' Alec—that was the first hurdle over. 'But I'll have to think about it. May I let you know later?'

He looked taken aback for a moment, and then pleased in a cautious sort of way. 'I suppose,' he said, 'that you might be washing your hair, or doing some other female thing that's mystifying to us poor males.'

He hasn't been out on a date for years, Veronica realised. She tilted back her head and chuckled. 'Nobody uses that corny old excuse any more,' she said gently. 'Most of us just wash our hair when we shower—it's no big deal.'

Alec raised a straight, thick eyebrow—it struck Veronica how different they were to Jeremy's narrow, arched ones. Alec's thin-lipped mouth quirked ironically.

'I do catch the commercials occasionally,' he said. 'I don't live in an ivory tower.'

It was the sort of put-down that until a few minutes ago would have made her or anybody in the firing line cringe, but now it just seemed amusing that her clever boss had had the last word as usual. An evening out with him might be just what she needed to take her mind off Jeremy.

Her headache had miraculously cleared and she suddenly felt on top of the world—elated. She said, 'Alec, I'd like to take you up on your invitation to dinner. What time should I be ready, and should I dress up or down?'

Alec inclined his head in a little bow. 'It's refreshing to meet a woman who can be direct. Time, eight o'clock. I'll pick you up. Dress on the sophisticated side.' And with a nod he turned on his heel and marched away down the corridor.

Veronica smiled at his retreating back. 'I seem doomed,' she murmured, 'to attract men who are forever walking away from me.'

The reception area was about half full. The waiting time was twenty minutes according to the display above the reception desk. Not bad, thought Veronica as she made her usual round of the patients, cubicles and staff. If we can keep that up, we'll have a nice easy day.

'And pigs might fly,' scoffed Dick an hour later when waiting time was up to an hour and a half and Veronica told him of her earlier wishful thinking.

He and Veronica were working on an elderly man who had fallen and cracked his head. He had fallen sideways and had a bad cut just above his ear which was bleeding profusely. He was also dazed and muddled and looked puzzled when Dick explained that he would have to have his head X-rayed.

'What'dya mean, X-rayed?' the man asked truculently, attempting to get off the couch.

It took both Dick and Veronica their combined strength to restrain him. They looked at each other over the old chap, now lying exhausted against the pillow. The truculence and irritability itself indicated possible brain damage, as did the sudden flurry of strength. They'd both seen it before.

'Because you've bumped your head badly, Mr Clark, and we need to see if there's any deeper damage.'

His eyes sharpened suddenly. 'Like to m' brain, you mean?'

Dick nodded. 'Best to make sure,' he said.

'Then get on with it,' the old man muttered. 'Might as well know the worst.'

Dick had the mobile X-ray machine brought to the department so that it could be done on the spot.

The X-ray revealed a depressed fracture of the skull with possible internal bleeding. A bed was found for Mr Clark in the CCU, the critical care unit. 'But don't send us up anyone else,' said the unit sister when Veronica phoned. 'That's our last bed.'

'That's what you always say,' said Veronica with a laugh. 'Can't make any promises, but thanks for taking Mr Clark. We still haven't been able to get hold of any family, but the police are trying to track them down.'

Having seen her patient safely on his way to CCU, Veronica did another check of the cubicles and Reception. Waiting time had stuck at an hour and a half.

'Chiefly,' explained Rebecca, when Veronica stopped to have a word, 'because domestic emergencies have been coming in thick and fast this morning. There's one in resus at the moment which the boss man is dealing with.'

The mention of Alec, to whom she hadn't given a

thought over the last hour so since she'd been helping out with the hands-on nursing, reminded Veronica of her date with him later and gave her a dart of pleasure. It would be quite an experience, dining with the hard man of the hospital and an even more dedicated bachelor than Jeremy.

She attended to a child with a burn on her hand and arm, not a bad one because the mother had done all the right things, keeping it immersed in ice cold water and strapping a bag of frozen peas to the burn area when she'd transported her daughter to hospital.

'You're a lucky girl, Lucy,' Veronica told the four-year-old, as she removed the bag of peas and the large square of thin cotton material beneath, to reveal a long bright pink burn mark on the inside of the plump little arm. 'Your mummy has been very clever, looking after your arm. It would have been much worse if she hadn't kept it cold.'

Lucy nodded her curly head. Her cheeks were tear-stained but she was now quite composed. 'Mummy explained why it had to be kept cold and I only cried a bit when I first burnt it, and then the cold stopped it hurting so much.'

Veronica smiled at the middle-aged woman who was standing unfussily beside the couch, holding Lucy's undamaged hand.

'Congratulations Mrs Carstairs, you've done a neat job on Lucy's hand and arm.' Gently she swabbed the red area with an antiseptic lotion. 'That's to keep it clean and prevent any infection getting in,' she explained to Lucy.

'Mummy said that you would do that,' replied Lucy proudly. 'She knows all about these things 'cos she's a nurse.'

Mrs Carstairs laughed. 'Was,' she said. 'Many moons ago.'

'Have you thought about taking it up again, even if it's just part time?' Veronica asked. 'We're chronically short of nurses.'

'Heavens, I couldn't begin to tackle all the gadgetry that you use now. I can manage a drip, pop in a catheter, take a temperature, and that's about it. It's fifteen years since I retired to have a family and a lot's happened in the medical world since then. And anyway, though the boys are fourteen and could take care of themselves for a time, Lucy needs me to be around, don't you, love?'

Lucy had obviously been following and understanding much of the conversation, for she said, 'You could be a nurse when I'm at playschool, Mummy.'

'What a brilliant suggestion,' said Veronica. She finished applying a light dressing to the burn area. 'There, that's all done. Try not to get it wet, love. Perhaps Mummy can find a big plastic bag to go over it when you have your bath.' She helped Lucy down from the couch and turned to Mrs Carstairs. 'Do give the nursing some thought. There are leaflets in main Reception about orientation courses to help people to return to nursing, and we have a play centre for up to ten-year-olds, so Lucy wouldn't be a problem.'

Mrs Carstairs's eyes lit up. 'Do you think that I might make a go of it?' She looked wistful. 'It would be lovely to do something useful again. I've missed nursing so much.'

'Go for it, you're just the sort of person we want,' assured Veronica. 'Keen and dedicated and trained on the concept of tender loving care.'

Veronica felt buoyed up for the rest of her shift. Nurses of Mrs Carstairs's calibre were just what Porthampton

University Hospital needed to back up its international reputation for expertise and research—perhaps one day they might lead the field for the excellence of their hands-on nursing.

She floated the idea past Alec that evening at dinner, when they were already mellowed by wine and a delicious starter of lightly fried whitebait.

So far, she reflected, the evening had gone well. Alec had arrived on the dot of eight in a taxi. 'When I manage to tear myself away from the hospital,' he'd said, with a definite sparkle in his dark brown eyes, 'I like to be able to enjoy my wine without fear of being breathalysed.'

Veronica had been surprised by his relaxed manner. There had been no sign of the stiff boss man. And his dinner suit and black tie suited him. He'd looked as if he was accustomed to wearing it.

'Oh, then you won't be able to stop for a drink,' she'd said, 'if you've got a taxi waiting.'

'No problem,' he'd replied. 'I have a running account with a company, the car is mine for as long as I want it. I'd love a drink before we start out.'

So he came into her flat and congratulated her on the dry sherry she offered him. For twenty minutes they talked of this and that without effort. Then he helped her on with the blue velvet wrap she had chosen to wear over the mid-calf-length slinky grey silk dress and escorted her to the waiting chauffeur-driven car.

He had been right to suggest sophistication, she realised, when he showed her into a discreet restaurant on the seafront a few miles along the coast from Porthampton. Everything about the inside was rich in an understated way. There were murals and tapestries on the walls, thick carpets beneath their feet and no prices on the menu.

The Old Thatched Barn had been a revelation and the home-produced food superb. Brownings, with its discreet front entrance opening onto the village street and catering to the international yachting fraternity was in a different class and specialised in fish dishes. It was impossible to compare the two restaurants, they were both excellent in their way.

Sheer luxury, Veronica thought, two nights in one week with two handsome men wining and dining me. What more could any woman want? *Just Jeremy*, whispered an inner voice. She squashed the voice and hoped that Alec hadn't noticed her flushed cheeks.

She said quickly, whilst they were waiting for the next course, 'Do you mind if we talk shop for a moment, or is it taboo?'

'Not at all,' he answered seriously. 'Medicine is, after all, our mutual source of interest.'

So she told him about Mrs Carstairs and how she thought that there must be a huge number of women like her—and wouldn't it be wonderful if they could build a reputation for the excellence of their hands-on nursing?

'They would be a buffer,' she said as their main course arrived, 'between doctors and officialdom and all the technical apparatus of today's hospital experience. People who are ill need—'

'Tender loving care,' said Alec. 'Yes, I get the message, Veronica.' He raised his glass of wine and touched it to hers. 'It's possible that if the powers that be think that there's good publicity in the idea, they might go for it. Leave it with me, I'll see what I can do.'

The rest of the evening was easy and comfortable and Veronica enjoyed herself immensely. It was midnight when Alec took her home. He said goodnight to her in the corridor outside her flat, brushing a kiss across her cheek.

What a nice man he is, she thought as she drifted into sleep. I wonder why he presents such an unfeeling face to the world…

## CHAPTER SIX

THE few days that Jeremy was away dragged interminably. The hospital, teeming with patients and staff, seemed to Veronica empty. Every moment she expected, hoped, to see Jeremy's tall figure come striding round a corner. Try as she might to dismiss his image, she couldn't. He was there in the back of her mind all the time. She wished that they'd talked more the other night—not parted on a sour note.

She and Alec hadn't spoken on a personal level since they'd dined together, and she thought on the third morning of Jeremy's absence that Alec was missing him, too, if his grim expression was anything to go by.

It was a busy morning in the resuscitation unit. She and several other medics and nurses were pulling out all the stops to keep alive and repair serious injuries to two dockyard workers. Alec was moving between the resus tables, supervising and offering advice.

The two men had been working on a liner in dry dock. They had been sitting one at each end of a cradle suspended over the side of the oceangoing ship, making superficial repairs to the hull, when the chains supporting the cradle had slipped, throwing them fifty feet below to the floor of the concrete basin. Both had been wearing hard hats, but one had been knocked off in the fall, and the man's face and head were in a terribly battered state. In addition, both legs were shattered and there were internal injuries.

The other man also had internal injuries, a fractured pelvis and possible spinal damage.

It took the team over an hour to tidy up both patients enough for them to be taken upstairs to the trauma unit.

As they were all stripping off plastic aprons and gloves, Alec moved to Veronica's side. 'May I have a word with you in my office, Sister?'

'Certainly,' said Veronica, ignoring Janice who rolled her eyes heavenward.

She followed Alec along the corridor.

He shut the door behind her as she entered the office and motioned to her to sit down.

'I found a message from Jeremy on my answerphone when I got home last night. He's coming back this evening. Apparently he's been trying to contact you, but without success.'

Veronica experienced a rush of pleasure just at the sound of Jeremy's name, and pleased surprise that he'd bothered to let her know through Alec. 'I haven't got an answering machine and I've been on duty or out with friends over the last couple of nights,' she explained.

Alec smiled. 'So you've already made some friends here in Porthampton.'

'Yes, and I've met up with a couple of people whom I trained with years ago.'

'The hospital world's a small one,' Alec said. 'Which brings me to another point. I met up with Rick Mannering and mentioned to him your thoughts on hands-on nursing.'

Veronica tried to concentrate on what Alec was saying, but in her mind she was already anticipating her meeting with Jeremy and she stared blankly at Alec. What did he mean? Who was he talking about?

Alec answered her unspoken bewildered thoughts. 'Sir

Richard Mannering, who is treasurer on the board of trustees,' he explained, a touch of dry humour in his voice. 'Of all the people on the board, it's his support we will need if we're to have any success with your clever idea—he holds the purse-strings. We dined together at our club the other night.'

His words struck home and she was suddenly alert. Of course, luring retired nurses back to do hands-on nursing, not to deal with too much high-tech stuff. Make Porthampton the leaders in the field with a school of hands-on nursing.

'But that's wonderful,' Veronica replied, treating him to one of her radiant smiles. 'I'd no idea that you would do anything so quickly.'

'I was brought up on all the old adages about early birds catching worms and don't put off till tomorrow what you can do today, a stitch in time, etc., etc. Anyway, we've engaged his interest.'

Remembering her father's business dealings, Veronica gave a short laugh. 'At the cost of an arm and a leg or at least a good dinner, I guess.'

Alec's lip curled sardonically. 'You could say that,' he agreed.

His phone rang at that moment, and Veronica took her leave. She could have hugged him, she thought, had Alec been the huggable sort.

Glad for once that there was a pile of paperwork to do, she shut herself away in her office for the rest of her shift and got stuck into it. But in spite of long practice and an iron determination to finish the job before going home, Jeremy would keep intruding on her mind.

*Jeremy!* He would be home tonight. Her body responded as it had recently started to do at the thought of seeing him. Her heart thumped uncomfortably hard, her pulses raced and the hairs on the back of her neck stood up, sending an icy shiver down her spine. How had it happened in such a short while? He had come back into her life and turned it upside down.

She sat in her chair in front of her desk, closed her eyes and hugged herself, letting herself imagine the luxury of being hugged by Jeremy as he'd embraced her the night before he'd gone away. His firmly muscled arms had pinioned her to his chest like bands of steel, surprising her by their strength.

And when he'd released her, he'd told her that their future was in her hands. 'I've bags of patience,' he'd said.

Patience! She thought that she understood about patience. She'd had patience, clinging onto hope when she'd been so desperately ill after the accident, and then over the following years, when it had appeared that nothing could be done to improve the scar round her eye; learning to live with it and get on with her life.

She detached her mind, unfolded her arms and began tackling the pile of papers that had to be dealt with. And rather to her shame, because she had never clock-watched, she looked forward to the end of her shift.

Veronica's phone was ringing as she opened the door of her flat and she raced to pick it up, her antennae telling her that it was Jeremy at the other end.

'Alec give you my message?' he asked, without preamble.

'Yes,' she murmured, too breathless to say more. It was heaven to hear his voice.

'I'm through London, so I should get back in an hour and a half or so. May I invite myself to a meal? Beans on toast will do as long as there's plenty of it.'

Excitement and anticipation made her stumble over her

words and she bubbled with laughter. 'Oh, I think we can do better than that.'

The thought of feeding him for some reason filled her with an excitement that she had never experienced before. For a modern, professional woman who believed in equality, in the kitchen as well as anywhere else, it was ludicrous—yet here she was, keen to show off her culinary skills to this man. It was extraordinary.

'I'm hungry,' he warned. 'Quantity rather than quality is what I need.'

'You can have both,' she said, and put the phone down before she made a bigger fool of herself.

A search through the freezer revealed what was referred to in the family as Granny's Special, or French Grandmama's Special as her mother called it, which sounded a bit more upmarket—layers of onions, mince, tomatoes, peppers, herbs and thinly sliced potatoes in a large flat dish. Cooking time about an hour and a bit but it could be left safely simmering for much longer.

'Perfect,' Veronica murmured, popping it into the middle of the oven. She would move it to the top to crisp up later. 'Now—pudding.' She glanced at the clock—she'd still got well over an hour. Baked apples—she'd bought cooking apples a few days ago, they'd only want coring. And…ice cream, brilliant. And starters? Melon and avocado marinated in sherry.

Such simple preparations left her with plenty of time to shower and wash her hair, but choosing what to wear took longer. It was ridiculous to be bothered about something so mundane when they were only eating at home, but somehow it seemed important to look *right*, create the impression that this was a special yet homely occasion.

In the end she settled for clingy jeans and a ribbed yellow polo-necked sweater, chunky amber necklace, a spicy perfume and discreet amber drop earrings. Her hair, brushed till it shone, hung like a red-blonde veil down one side of her face to conceal her scar, and was caught back on the other side by a jewelled Victorian comb.

Her doorbell buzzed as she was checking the oven—Jeremy! Someone must have let him in at the front entrance. She returned the dish to the oven and went to open the door.

Jeremy, his arms full of flowers, was leaning casually against the doorframe. 'Very domesticated,' he said dryly, glancing down at the oven gloves she had forgotten to remove.

Veronica was open-mouthed and speechless and motioned him into the sitting room. Everything about him took her by surprise—the flowers, the tweedy jacket, cord trousers and well polished brogues, and most of all his casual, upbeat manner and the fact that he looked so at home in the out-of-town gear.

She snapped her mouth closed and swallowed, but her voice sounded sexily husky when she spoke. She must get a grip on herself.

'*Country Life* to the life,' she drawled.

He laid the flowers down on a side table, after casting a quick look at the round table laid for supper. 'The conference was at a country house just outside York. Seemed a pity not to dress for the part.'

'But neither the jacket nor the shoes are new, they've been worn many times before...' What was she waffling on about?

'Sherlock-Holmsing, Veronica? Well, I do live in the country,' he said mildly, 'and I've got a few animals, so I'm entitled to look a bit rural if I want to, am I not?'

Veronica picked up the flowers and buried her face in them. What sort of animals, what sort of house? She didn't know whether she was on her head or her heels—this was another Jeremy she didn't know. She, who was normally cool and sophisticated, felt anything but.

'I'll find something to put these in and serve supper immediately as you're so hungry.' She waved a hand as she disappeared toward the kitchen. 'The bathroom's through there.'

Jeremy grinned—a wide schoolboy grin. His face lit up. 'As in wash your hands before you come to the table? You sound just like my mother. Sometimes she treats me as a twelve-year-old instead of a thirty-two-year-old.'

'Snap,' said Veronica briskly. 'That's my mother, too, always ordering me around—the iron lady, my mama.'

Was it his imagination, Jeremy wondered, or did he detect a note of bitterness in her voice?

She found a big ceramic jug in which to put the flowers, all blue and purple, mostly lilac and bluebells and an occasional yellow iris. She carried it through to the sitting room.

It was heavy. Jeremy took it from her. 'Where do you want it, love?'

'On the bureau, please.' She sniffed the heady scent as he put the vase down. 'These aren't from a garage forecourt,' she said. 'They're straight from a garden, there are even a few drops of rain on them from the last shower.'

He hung his head in mock shame. 'I was nearer to home than I let on when I phoned,' he said softly. 'I stopped off at my place to cut them for you. It's my way of apologising for my impulsive behaviour the other night. Am I forgiven?'

In a low voice, she murmured, 'What am I supposed to forgive, Jeremy?'

'My coming on too strong the other night, frightening you. I didn't mean that to happen.' His eyes were soft and gentle. 'But I'm not made of stone. You looked wonderful...tired, pale, vulnerable, and for once touchable. I felt that you needed me to hold you, support you—it had been a rough sort of day.'

That's precisely what she had wanted, and for the brief moments he had held her crushed against his chest she had felt safe and secure. So why had she begged him to release her when she should have been returning his embrace and offering him comfort? It had been a rough sort of day for both of them. She should have been there for him as he'd been for her.

Her breathing was so erratic that he must see the uneven rise and fall of her breasts beneath the ribbed wool of her sweater, she thought. She mustn't make the same mistake twice. He needed her reassurance again. He'd said that it was up to her how their relationship shaped up...well, she wanted it to grow and strengthen. No more would he be able to call her untouchable.

She stepped toward him, slipped her arms round his neck and pulled his head down until their lips could meet. 'Kiss me, Jeremy, please,' she whispered. 'Make love to me.'

He kissed her, at first very gently, small fluttery kisses on her mouth and face and trailing down her throat, then more fiercely, returning to her mouth, forcing her lips apart with his strong tongue.

Their tongues mingled and explored, and his hands slid up under her sweater and beneath her bra and his fingers teased her nipples until they were taut and erect.

Veronica sighed softly and let her own hands wander beneath his jacket and his waistcoat. Her fingers were a little clumsy as she eased his shirt out of the waistband of his trousers, and laid the palm of her hands against his flat abdomen, before sliding them up to his broad chest, and deliberately tweaking her fingers in the scattering of close curly hair.

Jeremy made a little hissing noise between his teeth then, giving her breasts a gentle squeeze, put her bra in place and slowly removed his hands from beneath her sweater.

He lifted his head and murmured against her mouth, a tinge of humour in his voice, 'Kissing I can do on an empty stomach, but making love is a definite no-no.'

She squashed the waves of disappointment that flowed over her and even managed a little chuckle as she drew herself away from him.

'Oh, well, in that case,' she said breathily, 'We must feed the brute.' She pointed to the white wine in the ice cooler. 'Can you pour it out, please?' she murmured. 'I'll bring in the starters.'

They both made a huge effort at polite conversation as they ate. They worked their way through the melon and avocado, which Jeremy pronounced 'refreshing' and then through 'Granny's Special', which he thought was out of this world. He had two helpings. And the baked apples and ice cream were 'perfect'.

Veronica wasn't able to distinguish one course from the other as she tried to unravel her thoughts.

When Jeremy had said that he couldn't make love on an empty stomach, had he been implying that when he'd eaten he *would* make love to her? Her heart skittered around in her chest—no, he wouldn't be that calculating. For whatever reason, she felt in her bones that he hadn't intended to make love to her tonight. And if that were so, then the sooner she brought the evening to an end and salvaged what was left of her pride the better.

Sensible decision, but how to put it into action? She

could hardly turf him out the minute that they'd had their coffee.

At that moment, Jeremy leaned across the table and clinked his glass to hers. She met his dark eyes over the rims of the touching glasses. 'I've missed you, Veronica,' he said, his voice rich and deep. 'Missed you desperately.'

With an effort, she tidied away her tumultuous thoughts, and asked evenly, 'Then why did you go away, Jeremy? Alec said that you were going to give the conference a miss.'

'I was, but I needed to get away from here, and from you, and think.'

Veronica wrapped both hands round her glass, and propped her arms on the table. 'Am I allowed to know what you needed to think about?'

'You and me,' he said, but didn't expand further.

She had to battle to keep her temper. 'Is that all?' she asked, her voice cold.

'For the moment, yes,' he replied. 'Please, bear with me, Veronica,' he added softly, 'for the time being.'

It was unusual to have him plead for anything. Was it her imagination, or did he look and sound less sure of himself than usual?

'I'll fetch the coffee,' she said.

They talked over coffee, rescuing the remnants of the evening in civilised conversation.

The conference had been rather dull, Jeremy told her, so he'd skipped several of the lectures and gone walking instead.

'Lovely country round York, do you know it?' he asked.

Veronica shook her head, quite unaware how the last of the setting sun slanting through the window caused it to glint as if it were on fire. Jeremy caught his breath and resisted stroking it.

'No,' she said, 'I don't know that part of the world at all.'

'I'll take you there some time,' he said, almost absent-mindedly. 'You'll like it—and you must see the Minster, definitely worth a visit.'

Did he realise what he'd said? Veronica wondered. 'I'll take you there'—sure of her acquiescence. Her stomach churned, her cheeks paled then flushed, and for the second—or maybe the third—time since he'd arrived, she was speechless. She didn't know whether to be angry or flattered, or how to respond. No man had ever puzzled and surprised her as this man did.

Jeremy was standing up and saying something…

Veronica lifted her head and stared at him. 'I'm sorry, what did you say?'

'Shall we finish our coffee over there?' He indicated the chairs by the flower-filled fireplace. 'We might sit there and be more comfortable.'

'Yes, of course.' She got up and wandered to one of the chairs by the fireplace. I can't take this in, she thought. What does he mean? Why is he making plans as if we're an item, as if there's a definite future for us together? How am I going to handle this?

Everything in her world, just as she was settling into the University Hospital, was changing, getting away from her, leaving her feeling as if she were on a slippery slope to an unknown destination.

She stared into space and only became aware of Jeremy when the fragrance of the coffee mingled with his particular masculine scent.

'You were a million miles away,' he said softly. 'I've

topped up your coffee.' He placed her cup and saucer on a small table beside her. 'And you look…bothered.'

Playing host, he offered cream and brown sugar. She poured in cream, but shook her head at the sugar. 'Yes, bothered,' she confirmed, 'and puzzled and—'

'And not very happy apparently. What's suddenly gone wrong, love?' Jeremy sat down opposite her and helped himself to sugar and cream. His eyes were gentle and enquiring.

He had removed his jacket. The soft wool shirt and tie and waistcoat were all part of the country gentleman image. Not a hollow image, though, she reminded herself. He *was* a country gentleman when he wasn't being a consultant surgeon, whatever his humble beginnings.

*Humble beginnings!* She shook her head to rid herself of the pernicious phrase.

He stirred his coffee and said softly, 'So why don't you tell me what it's all about, Veronica.'

Her thoughts seemed to be fragmented. If only she could get them together. She sipped her coffee and raised her head and looked straight into his dark eyes. 'I don't know where to start,' she said, and thought, Why are we talking about me when it ought to be about him?

'Try saying the first thing that comes into your head—it can work, you know. What, or who, are you thinking of at this moment?'

'Alec.' The word popped into her mind and out of her mouth.

It was impossible to tell whether Jeremy was surprised. He wore his impassive surgeon's face. 'What do you want to know about Alec?'

'Where he fits in. I know that you and he are friends, but there's something else. When we first met—met again—you inferred that it was because of Alec, but you were bound to secrecy. Would it help if I told you that he took me out to dinner the other night?'

His face lost its impassiveness, which was replaced by a pleased expression. 'Well, good for Alec. It releases me from a promise of keeping silent. He was very keen that I should look at your scar and assess whether I could do anything for you. But, true to form, he didn't want you to know that he was instrumental in bringing it to my attention, but that was before it turned out that we had known each other in the past. That somewhat blurred matters.'

'Why?' Veronica suddenly felt very alert. All sorts of ideas were beginning to slot into place.

Jeremy had some idea of what was going on in Veronica's head. Her bright mind was putting together the bits of the puzzle. She'd noticed, he guessed, without reading any significance into it, the number of times she'd found Alec glancing at her. Now it was making some kind of sense.

'Why did things become blurred?' she asked.

'Because I realised when we sat on the seat in the courtyard, renewing our acquaintance, that I was still as fascinated by you as I had been at school. Only now there's a difference. I no longer suffer from acne and I'm a grown man and it has put us on a level playing field. And Alec guessed as much and didn't know whether it was going to help or hinder my chance of persuading you to have surgery.'

Veronica shook her head. 'No, it hasn't put us on a level playing field—it's reversed our roles completely. I'm the disfigured one now, you're the handsome, all-powerful Prince Charming. You hold all the aces, Jeremy.'

Did she really feel herself so disfigured? Hadn't the fact

that he was clearly in love with her done anything to restore her self-confidence? Working all day and every day with disfigured patients, it had taught him that healing the physical scars was a damn sight easier than repairing the psychological ones, but…

'Jeremy?'

Veronica's voice jogged him out of his reverie and he scrambled his thoughts together. What had she said—that he held all the aces?

'I don't, you know, hold all the aces,' he argued sharply. 'Falling in love with you all over again is a two-edged sword and the last thing that I wanted to do. When Alec set the ball rolling, I wondered briefly if he was in love with you, which would have given me a sound reason to hold myself in check, but he soon disabused me of that idea…'

Veronica gave a deep, throaty chuckle. 'I should think so, too,' she said, suddenly feeling much better, much more herself. 'Alec was a wonderful host and I look forward to dining with him again, but Alec as a lover…I think not. I don't mean that unkindly, I simply mean that Alec is a dedicated bachelor, and I respect him for it.'

She almost added, And I'm a dedicated bachelor woman.

'Well, you read him better than I did, although I should have sussed him out. But the fact remains that Alec being out of the running for your affections left me with no defence against your beauty, so much enhanced by the new you, the gentle, caring you. I should have backed off then, but I didn't, so you're stuck with me and my love, Veronica.'

He smiled a glancing smile at her and then looked at the silver carriage clock on the mantlepiece and stood up. 'It's getting late, so I'd better be off.'

'But you can't go now, it isn't that late.' Veronica stood up, too, anxious to detain him. 'And we haven't resolved anything.'

Jeremy took a step toward her and cupped her face in his hands, deliberately drawing her veil of hair back from the scarred side of her face. He kissed the scar, her forehead, nose and cheeks, and finally her mouth. Veronica couldn't stop herself flinching.

He said softly, 'Alec was right. Until we've sorted this for you...' he ran his finger round her eye '...you won't be ready for a serious relationship, and *I*, my dearest, darling Veronica, am only interested in marriage.'

'M-m-marriage! ' she stammered.

'Marriage,' Jeremy murmured, his thumbs stroking her cheeks. He kissed the tip of her nose again and then her trembling lips. 'Call me old-fashioned, but this is something that I feel strongly about—if two people love each other, and I'm talking about love here, not just sexual attraction, unless there's a legal reason not to do so, why not get married?'

His voice and his deep blue eyes were velvet soft, his hands, cupping her face, were gentle but firm.

Veronica struggled for breath and self-control. Marriage! She must have misheard—but she hadn't. But how could he mean marriage and commitment when they'd only just met again? And he seemed so sure, positive. She was attracted to him, and it wasn't just superficial attraction, but she was a long way from being ready to commit herself to a relationship of any kind.

She said breathlessly, 'I'm not ready for this, Jeremy, I need time, much, much more time. Please, don't push me.'

He lowered his hands to her shoulders and down her upper arms and then pulled her close to his chest.

'I won't push you, love. Take all the time that you need. Just remember that I'm here for you always.' His hands caressed her back and then slid down her spine to cup her buttocks. 'I love you, Veronica, and will go on loving you always.'

He held her close for a few moments, and then released her. 'I must go,' he said, and left the flat as suddenly as he had a few nights ago.

And again she listened to his footsteps receding along the hall, before moving to the window to watch him drive away.

This time he looked up and, seeing her silhouetted against the lamplight, lifted his hand in a farewell salute as he turned into the lane.

Veronica went to bed feeling muddled and despondent, aware that she hadn't handled the evening very well. She had encouraged Jeremy to come and had pulled out all the stops to make him welcome, making it obvious that she was pleased to see him. But it had somehow misfired.

Jeremy had read into it more than she'd intended, and had started talking marriage, which was the last thing she was looking for. His exit speech about only being interested in marriage had been a shock. Wasn't it the woman who usually sought that kind of commitment? Another instance of role reversal, she thought.

And on that thought she pulled the duvet over her head and ran her finger round her lips.

'Good night, Jeremy,' she murmured. 'Sleep well, my love.'

# CHAPTER SEVEN

VERONICA woke early the next morning in a positive frame of mind. She wouldn't spend time bemoaning last evening, she would sort out this problem of how to come to terms with the situation between herself and Jeremy.

There was no doubt that she was strongly attracted to him, and had admitted to herself that she was more than half in love with him—her body language told her that. But marriage! He'd shaken her to the core when he'd spoken so forcefully of it last night. She had long ago given up any idea of marriage or a long-term relationship.

No way could she face the thought of being seen before she had camouflaged her scar each day, and that's what it would mean if she shared her bed with anyone on a serious basis.

'Bit extreme, isn't it?' her best friend from her school days had commented when Veronica had announced her intention of never marrying for that reason. 'Honestly, Vee, your scar isn't nearly as bad as you imagine. You're just overly sensitive about it because you've always had a flawless complexion. Anyway…' Liz had shrugged '…when the right guy comes along, you won't mind if he sees your scar or not, and neither will he.'

Veronica had been sceptical but had allowed, as she'd got older, that there might be some truth in that. But was Jeremy that man? she mused as she showered and put on old jeans and a sweater and let herself out of the house. A brisk walk along the bridle path that led from the top of the lane across the downs would clear her head and enable her to do some hard thinking.

It was a perfect March morning, all blue skies and dazzling golden sunshine. Dew sparkled on the rabbit-cropped turf of the downs and the birds were singing their hearts out.

Far below, the sea sparkled and the ships in Porthampton harbour looked like toys. Already the dockyard was busy, with small tugs buzzing about and a couple of huge cranes moving with stately slowness, swinging heavy loads across the sky.

Looking down on the huge sprawl of the city with its long coastline, she wondered fleetingly how the two men who had been repairing the liner were doing. Now that Jeremy was back, would he be operating on the dockyard worker whose face had been so badly smashed? She sighed and smiled wryly. Jeremy wouldn't stay out of her thoughts for long.

The sun was already warm. It would be April soon and a warm April was being forecast—in fact, the weather people were talking about a very hot summer.

Veronica walked briskly to match her mood, breathing in deeply, sampling the scent of the dewy grass and occasional patches of sweet-smelling thyme that she crushed underfoot. Her long untethered hair shimmered in the sunshine. She felt free and relaxed and, although she had meant to think, her mind was empty.

After a quarter of an hour, she found a little depression beside the bridle path which trapped the sunshine. She stretched out on the grass, uncaring of the dewy damp, and closed her eyes. The warm sun caressed her eyelids and cheekbones…

The rhythmic thud of hoofbeats woke her and she rolled over onto her stomach to watch the rider approach. He looked huge, coming from the east, silhouetted against the early morning sunshine. A large man on a large horse.

Not until he was a few yards away did Veronica realise that it was Jeremy.

Jeremy recognised her at the same moment and reined in.

'Veronica!' he exclaimed.

At the same moment, in the same surprised tone, she said, 'Jeremy!'

There wasn't time for her usual reaction to his presence. She scrambled to her feet as Jeremy slid down from the saddle of the large black horse. The magnificent beast stood quietly, though trembling a little after his gallop, as Jeremy dismounted.

How exactly right he looks, thought Veronica, as much at ease in riding breeches and a safety helmet as in a conservative suit or casual wear.

She avoided meeting his eyes and moved across to stroke the horse's nose.

'Oh, what a beauty you are,' she said. The horse tossed his head gently and snorted in a pleased fashion. Veronica blew softly across his nostrils. 'What's his name?' she asked Jeremy, only slightly turning her head so that she didn't have to face him fully. After last night, she couldn't imagine what they would say to each other. It was a relief to have the horse as a distraction.

'Officially it's Campion, but I always call him Beauty.'

'As in Black Beauty?'

'What else? I can't remember when my mother first read the book to me before I could read myself, but I know that we both cried buckets.'

'So did I,' said Veronica, with a dreamy smile, 'every time I read it. But I'm surprised you read it. I always thought of it more as a girl's book than a boy's.'

Jeremy shrugged. 'I was brought up by a single mum. It had been a favourite of hers when she was young. She was a great reader and introduced me to a lot of authors I would have missed in a more conventional household.'

Remembering, he stared into the distance for a moment, his midnight blue eyes soft and dreamy, then added cheerfully, 'Of course, I liked the boys' adventure stuff, too, all goodies and baddies and bang, bang, you're dead, and I was hooked on science fiction. Couldn't wait to get my space comic each week. Mum used to read it as well, and we raced each other to the door when it was delivered. But my mother's taste in literature has stayed with me and I read almost anything I can lay my hands on these days.'

Jeremy moved round to the other side of Beauty's nose and fished a carrot out of his pocket. The horse crunched on it enthusiastically. Veronica didn't say a word, afraid to break the flow of reminiscences, but continued to stroke Beauty's nose. This opportunity to learn more about Jeremy was too good to miss.

He was stroking Beauty's nose too, and occasionally their fingers touched, but he carried on speaking as if he hadn't noticed. 'Personally, I think it's a pity that more men don't read a few books written for or by women. Perhaps they would understand them better if they did...in fact, understand people better.'

This time, Veronica looked straight at him. 'What a refreshing remark to hear from a man, especially a man who's—'

'Woman-proof,' he put in with a sly grin.

Veronica blushed. 'I never did quite go along with that idea when I met up with you again. You're too assured and sophisticated, and I know that it's a deliberate policy to appear not to notice women.'

Jeremy nodded. 'Yep, a bachelor in the female-dominated hospital environment doesn't stand a chance. Although in the beginning, before I got used to having shed my acne, it was self-preservation. I was scared of being turned down if I tried to make a date. Psychological scars go deep, as you know, Veronica.'

Her hand went up beneath the curtain of hair, to the left side of her face.

He looked at his watch, uttered an expletive and swung himself up into the saddle, towering above her. 'Got to get to work, lots to catch up on.' He leaned down and, with his riding crop, lifted her hair. 'Let me look at it some time, Veronica, please, so that you can really live again.'

Then, turning Beauty around to face the way he had come, he tapped the animal's flanks, which were gleaming in the sunshine, and trotted away without a backward glance.

Veronica fumed as she walked home and was still fuming when she went on duty at ten. How dared he make remarks like that? 'Really live again.' What the devil did he mean by that? She was living a perfectly satisfactory life, thank you, without his help. And he wasn't an exactly integrated person himself, was he? Still nervous about making dates for fear of rejection.

No, honesty compelled her to admit that this wasn't quite true. He had explained why he kept a low profile, and it was justified. Unless he was interested in one-night stands, which he'd made it clear that he wasn't, as a bachelor he was an easy target for predatory females.

Some of her fury with him evaporated as she started work. She was doing a ten a.m. to midnight shift today, to allow her night sister counterpart to go to some family do. This was one of the things she enjoyed about being virtually her own boss—she could come and go as she pleased as long as the department was covered. It made for brilliant working relations with her colleagues.

'I owe you,' Bella Courtney said when Veronica agreed to do an extended duty period. 'Pay you back any time.'

Veronica did her usual round of the cubicles and reception area immediately she went on duty and, as she'd expected, everywhere was already almost full. Waiting time was at forty-five minutes. Alec was out and about, making his presence felt, even though there were no acute emergencies for him to deal with.

'Ah, good morning, Sister,' he greeted Veronica, his eyes bright. He was almost smiling. He glanced at his watch and clicked his tongue. 'You enjoyed a lie-in, I presume? Well deserved, of course, after the last few days' heavy workload.'

Veronica dazzled him with a smile. 'What, on a morning like this? No, I took a brisk walk on the downs. It was wonderful.' Of course it had been wonderful—Jeremy had come riding out of the east and they'd talked. Her heartbeat quickened. And then he'd spoiled it by being overbearing and commenting on her lifestyle.

The nerve of the man. And here was Alec Masterson, making assumptions and wearing a patronising smile.

Why was it that so many men seemed to automatically assume that they had the right to patronise women? Even Jeremy, who'd had a less conventional upbringing than usual.

Between these two autocratic men she suddenly felt that she was being squeezed. Both seemed to think that she needed looking after. Well, she was no nineteenth-century female, a prisoner to masculine authority. She would decide if and when she needed help.

It was hard not to be flattered by their attentions, but she wasn't looking for flattery, she wanted friendship with them both. Perhaps more than friendship with Jeremy, but on her terms. No live-in relationship. She meant to stick to her vow made long ago, at least for the time being.

The fact that Jeremy had made it plain last night that hopping into bed with her would be anathema to him wouldn't persuade her to change her mind. In spite of what he'd said, he would have to accept that it was all that would be on offer if he wanted to make love to her.

So it was a reversal of the male-female role. Most women wanted commitment, most men a casual affair. It was something he would have to come terms with.

She was aware that Alec was watching her with that slight smile hovering round his mouth as these thoughts whizzed through her head. It triggered off an idea—why not bring the two men face to face in her presence and tell them how she felt, that she was her own woman and quite capable of looking after herself?

She said quickly and quietly, 'When you have a minute, Alec, may I have a word, please, in your office?'

Unruffled as ever by the sudden request, he nodded. 'Barring emergencies, in ten minutes.'

'Fine,' replied Veronica, and moved away to have a word with Rebecca at the reception desk.

Rebecca was having a problem with a tough middle-aged man in dirty working clothes, who was being aggressive and difficult and demanding to jump the queue.

He was waving a hand swathed in a blood-soaked bandage under Rebecca's nose. 'Look at this,' he shouted. 'Bloody hand's nearly falling off and I've been waiting hours, and you just let that woman through though she's only just come in.'

'She had a sick child with her, and it's our policy to see children first,' Rebecca was explaining.

'Damned kids. Why should they have priority? I'm in agony here.' He shook his good fist threateningly at Rebecca.

Veronica slipped quietly in beside him and took hold of his wrist, knowing that he could easily shake her off if he wished but reckoning on surprise to stop him.

It did. He jerked his head round and looked into her steel grey eyes. 'I can call Security and have you removed,' she said, her voice as steely as her eyes. 'Or you can go and sit down over there…' she pointed to an empty chair '…and wait until you're called.'

He looked as if he were going to argue, then, recognising the voice of authority, suddenly deflated like a burst balloon. 'It's just that it's so damned painful and I've got to get back to work or they'll dock me pay.'

'Did you injure your hand at work?' asked Veronica, her voice gentler now.

'Yes.'

'How?'

'Picking up a broken bottle that was amongst the rubble. I'm with a demolition gang working round the corner in Elm Street.'

'And you weren't issued with protective gloves?' He shook his head. 'Then there's no way they can dock your pay. In fact, they may owe you compensation. We'll give you a certificate to confirm that you were here, receiving treatment, and if you want to take it further we can back you up.'

The man looked scared. 'I can't afford to lose this job,' he said. 'I've only just started with them.'

'Well, that's up to you, but you know where we are if you want back-up.'

'Thanks.'

Rebecca thanked her, too. 'Don't know how you do it,' she said. 'You should have been a diplomat.'

Veronica rolled her eyes. 'Heaven forbid,' she said with a laugh. 'I'm off now to have a word with Mr Masterson. Page his office if you want me.'

'Will do.'

She knocked firmly at Alec's door and was invited to enter in clipped tones. He was sitting at his desk, his chin resting on his hands, but started to rise when she entered.

'No, please, don't get up,' she said. 'May I?' she added, indicating a chair on the opposite side of the desk.

He nodded and sank back down onto his chair. 'Please, do.'

Veronica sat down with a smile. 'Alec, I'd like to invite you to dinner one evening as a thank you for wining and dining me the other day.'

'My dear Veronica, you don't have to thank me, but I'd love to spend another evening in your company. The other night we ran out of time rather than conversation. I'd like to make up for that.'

His stilted, old-fashioned phrasing unnerved her a little.

She said quickly, 'I need several possible dates when you're free...' she pulled a small diary from her uniform pocket '...as I'm inviting someone else and all our free evenings must coincide.'

'So it's not to be a tête-à-tête?'

'No, but I hope you'll enjoy it just the same, Alec.'

He smiled. 'I'm sure that I shall. Thank you for inviting me, I look forward to it.' He got his out his diary and they pencilled in a few dates over the next couple of weeks.

She was getting up to leave when Alec's phone jangled.

It was a red alert, an RTA, two adults two children, ETA ten minutes. They would both be needed in resus.

It was a long, tiring morning into afternoon, with no let-up. All four admissions were badly injured. The car in which they'd been travelling had been in collision with a huge container lorry that had jackknifed in front of them. This much they had found out from the police who had accompanied the ambulances to the hospital.

The patients were all unconscious and unable to give any information, but according to his licence the car driver's name was Roger Penn and it was presumed that those with him were his wife and two children. They came from Shrewsbury and the police there were contacting neighbours for further information.

A paediatrician was called down to check on the two small children. Both had internal injuries and the little girl head injuries, too. Both were given CT scans and sent up to the trauma unit after the A and E team had done what they could for them.

Everyone knew that it was touch and go for the small girl, and they continued working on the parents and the driver of the container lorry in a subdued frame of mind. Five critically injured people in one accident. It was a sobering thought.

The driver of the huge vehicle that had jackknifed had a stove-in chest and broken ribs, and one or more of the ribs had punctured his lung. Air was building up in the pleural cavity and a suction tube was inserted and would remain *in situ* for several days, draining out the air so the lung could expand.

Roger Penn had severe abdominal injuries and was haemorrhaging. It took a long time for Alec to find the blood vessel causing the bleeding and seal it off, and in spite of trying to make up the loss by infusing many litres of blood, the man remained at death's door.

He was transferred to the trauma unit a short time later for the expert care that they could give him, but the outlook was pretty grim.

Mrs Penn, amongst other injuries, had a fractured pelvis caused by a fractured femur, which the force of the car ramming into the jackknifed lorry had driven up into the pelvic cavity. She was in a lot of pain, hovering on the edge of consciousness and muttering incoherently. Veronica rather hoped that she wouldn't regain full consciousness immediately and realise that she and her family had been involved in a horrific accident.

Alec gave her a shot of diamorphine which diminished the pain and had the effect of keeping her semi-conscious for a little longer.

The orthopaedic surgeon Alec sent for decided that he would operate on her badly fractured femur as soon as a theatre was available. There were a lot of pieces of bone to be put together and a danger that infection might set in if it wasn't attended to urgently. Meanwhile they would take further X-rays of the pelvis to make sure that there was no damage to any abdominal organs.

At two-thirty Mrs Penn was transferred to the orthopaedic wing.

It was three o'clock before Veronica was able to leave the resuscitation room, and she disposed of her plastic gloves and apron as fast as she could, dumping them in the bin and hurrying out to avoid conversation with Alec or anyone else. She desperately needed to get out and breathe some fresh air. She still had a long stint ahead of her, another nine hours before she went off duty.

Because she'd left the house in a temper that morning after her encounter with Jeremy, she'd forgotten to make sandwiches. Remembering how low on blood sugar she had got the previous week when she hadn't taken time to eat, she popped into the cafeteria to pick up something, and found herself queuing behind Jeremy.

She almost slid away without speaking, but instead prodded his back. 'What are you doing here?' she hissed. 'Slumming it? Why aren't you in the consultants' dining room?'

'Two reasons,' he said calmly. 'One, I didn't want to bump into Alec—I heard you'd been working flat out in A and E, and there was a good chance he might be taking a late lunch—and, two, I need some fresh air.'

'So do I,' agreed Veronica fervently. 'Oh, boy, do I need fresh air.'

Jeremy piled sandwiches and apples and bananas onto his tray and took her tray from her. 'This'll be enough for both of us,' he said. 'Come on, I know a short cut to a little beach near here.'

Balancing the tray on one hand, he took her hand with the other and Veronica, taken by surprise, allowed herself to be led along corridors and out through a back door of the hospital.

The door was locked, but Jeremy had a key. He winked. 'Friends in high places,' he murmured.

'This is all very cloak and dagger,' Veronica muttered breathlessly, trying to keep up with his long strides as they crossed a rough-looking field.

Rumour had it that the trust planned to extend the hospital here at some future date, but at the moment it was uncut grass fringed by a copse of trees. Surprisingly, an overgrown path led through the trees, past a derelict building, ending, as he'd promised, in a tiny, pebbly beach, lapped by the sea and bathed in sunshine.

There was a little projection protruding into the water with a platform at the end.

Jeremy steered her along the wooden jetty to the platform.

'Long ago, this was an old timber wharf,' he explained. 'The tree trunks used for mast-making and other things were unloaded here onto small barges which meandered along the river through the city and linked up with the canal west of the town and on to the sawmills. It hasn't been used for donkey's years, and as you can see, it's deserted.'

'Heaven be praised,' said Veronica, lifting her face to the sun. 'Fresh air and no people.'

'What—don't I count as people?' Jeremy asked, pulling a droll face.

She laughed and blushed a delicate rose. 'Today, you're special people, because you've provided all this.' She waved her hand out over the water as they sat down on the wooden platform which was warm and dry.

Jeremy took off his jacket, rolled up his shirtsleeves and loosened his tie, and Veronica kicked off her shoes and wiggled her toes.

'This,' she said feelingly, 'is heaven after the stuffiness and noise of A and E. Thank you for bringing me here, Jeremy. How did you find it?'

He grinned. 'An old gentleman I treated a while back described where it was. He was a logger many moons ago.' He teased the tip of her nose with his forefinger. 'This will be our secret, understood?' Veronica nodded. 'You reveal its whereabouts to anyone on pain of death,' he added with mock sternness. 'As far as I know, nobody else ever comes here.'

'Not even Alec?'

'Not even Alec. We're not joined at the hip, you know. Here…' He handed her a sandwich. 'Chicken and ham.'

She took it from him and bit into it hungrily. 'Brilliant. It's good.'

'You've beautiful teeth,' Jeremy said, surprising her. 'Small and even. I remember admiring them when we did *A Midsummer Night's Dream* together all those years ago.'

He bit into his own sandwich, which triggered off a memory for Veronica. 'And you always had nice teeth,' she recalled. 'It was the one thing, that and your voice…' She trailed off. 'Sorry.'

Jeremy patted her arm. 'Don't be. I'm glad that you found one or two redeeming features about me. It must have been ghastly, having to do love scenes with me and my acne.'

They munched on their sandwiches in silence for a few minutes, both remembering. And then Veronica asked, 'How did you get rid of your spots so successfully? There isn't a mark on your face.' Tentatively she touched his arm. 'You don't mind my asking, do you?'

He covered her hand with his and met her concerned grey eyes with his dark ones. 'Veronica, love…' His voice was husky. 'Haven't you figured it out yet that I don't mind you asking anything of me, absolutely anything?' He leaned forward and kissed her hard on her mouth, the chicken on his lips mingling with hers. 'Mmm, that tastes good,' he said, running the tip of his tongue round her lips.

It was an incredibly sexy gesture, feather-light, making her shiver from top to toe and her taut breasts rise and fall rapidly as if she had been running hard. He withdrew his tongue but kept his face only inches from hers. His eyes were midnight blue velvet that she wanted to sink into. He lay back on the warm boards and pulled her down with him.

'I want to make love to you,' he whispered. 'I've wanted to make love to you for years.'

'I want to, too,' she murmured, 'but we can't, not here. Somebody might come.' What am I saying? she thought. Isn't this exactly what I want—love, sex, no commitment? So why not? He said that nobody ever comes here…

Jeremy crushed her to him for an instant, the whole length of his body moulded to hers. Then slowly he let her go. His breathing was harsh. He rolled away from her and sprang to his feet. 'No, you're right, nothing hole in corner for you. Sorry—shouldn't have done that. Like I said this morning, it's marriage or nothing for you and me.'

Veronica lay frozen, unable to move for a moment, staring up at him. Then she scrambled to her feet, shrugging away the hand he offered her. Through stiff lips, she uttered one word very forcefully. *'Nonsense!'*

He frowned. 'What do you mean, nonsense? I'm offering you marriage and you're rejecting it?'

Still looking him straight in the eye, she felt around for her shoes with her toes and edged them closer. 'Yes,' she said, without embroidery.

Jeremy took hold of her shoulders. 'Because of this obsession with this scar,' he said.

'No,' she replied, adding honestly, 'Well, not only that. It's because of your obsession with marriage. I don't want that, not yet anyway. For God's sake, Jeremy, this is the twenty-first century, we're two grown people, we would be consenting adults, you wouldn't be taking advantage of me. I'm not going to scream rape or broken promises if it doesn't work out.'

He crouched down and aligned her shoes with her

stockinged feet, then took hold of her slender ankles one at a time and guided her feet into her uniform shoes. His fingers felt cool and strong.

His hand wandered to the tray with the fruit piled on it. He picked up a rosy apple and polished it against his chest. 'Here…' He pressed it to her mouth. 'Munch on that and think about what I've said, what we've both said. Perhaps we do both have obsessions.'

The tension and anger drained out of her and, laughing, she nibbled at the apple and then brushed the nibbled bit against his lips. Her grey eyes twinkled like pearls. 'Isn't that my line?' she said on a laugh. 'Isn't it Eve who tempts Adam?'

He bit deliberately into the apple and masticated the firm flesh slowly. 'Adam certainly started something,' he murmured, 'by falling into temptation.'

He gathered up the remnants of their picnic, scattering the leftover sandwiches on the platform and on the water. Gulls that had been circling overhead swooped down and scooped up the floating crusts, and a young starling appeared out of nowhere and feasted on the dry crumbs on the platform.

Jeremy stuffed the rest of the fruit in his jacket pocket and tucked the empty tray under his arm. 'Come on, love,' he said, taking Veronica's hand. 'Once more into the breach.'

## CHAPTER EIGHT

'LIZ, it's Vee.'

'I'd know those dulcet tones anywhere. About time you phoned your best friend. How long have you been there now—six, seven weeks?'

'Nearly nine, actually, and if you will go off on these long safaris without leaving a forwarding address, how am I supposed to contact you?'

'Pigeon post.' Liz laughed. 'But I take your point. I only got back late last night and I'm shivering. Edinburgh seems very grey. The colours in—'

'Liz, must interrupt. Any other time you know how I love to have a blow-by-blow description of your travels before the rest of the world sees the film, but I've got a bit of a crisis on.'

'*Crisis?* That doesn't sound like you, you're so cool, calm and collected.'

'Hmm, not at the moment I'm not. Liz, do you remember Jeremy Grant—he played Oberon to my Titania at school? It was his last term.'

'The spotty youth for whom you had intense contempt? Yes, I remember him.'

Veronica winced at her friend's description. 'That's the one. Well, he's here at the Porthampton, the youngest plastic surgeon in the hospital and possibly in the country—he's brilliant.'

'Still spotty?'

'No. He's rather handsome actually.'

'And you've fallen for him.'

'Ye-es, I think so. He wants to marry me, Liz. Asked me right out of the blue. But I made a vow, you probably don't remember...'

'Of course I remember. I thought it was a whacky vow to make then, and I still do—is that what's holding you back from saying yes?'

'Partly, and partly because I'd like more time to get to know him, know him as he is now.'

'So what's stopping you?'

'He won't enter into a casual affair. I've offered, but he's adamant—no sex till marriage.'

'Good Lord, is he some kind of a freak or a saint? I don't think I've ever met a guy not prepared to hop under the duvet.'

'No, he's certainly not a freak or a saint, I've proof of that.' She felt herself go pink, remembering their body-to-body embrace on the beach last week. There had been nothing saintlike about that embrace. 'But he has the reputation for being woman-proof. His explanation for pretending not to notice women for the last couple of years or so is a deliberate pose to ward off predatory females.'

'Sounds reasonable. Does he know about your scar?'

'Yes, he wants to examine it, possibly operate to improve it. You see, Liz, he feels partly responsible for it...'

Suddenly it all came pouring out, about Greece and the earthquake and the fact that Jeremy had been there, but had walked away and had had feelings of guilt about that episode ever since.

'He has suggested that fate has thrown us together again so that he can right a wrong.'

'And you think that maybe triggered off his proposal?'

Veronica shook her head, forgetting that Liz couldn't see her. 'No, not really, but...'

'There's more to this confession?'

'Yep, there's Alec.'

'Alec?'

Veronica explained that Alec was her boss and Jeremy's close friend, and was nicknamed 'The Tin Man' because supposedly he was without a heart, but she had proof that he wasn't that.

'I sense a but,' said Liz. 'Are we talking the eternal triangle here? Jeremy and Alec?'

'No way. Alec is a bachelor to the core, unlike Jeremy who's only putting on an act. But both he and Jeremy seem to think that I need taking care of, and they're absolutely stifling me between them. I don't want to hurt either of them, and I certainly don't want to do or say anything to cause problems between them—they are great friends.'

'So how are you going to resolve it?'

'*That*,' replied Veronica soberly, 'is the billion-dollar question. Any ideas?'

'Well, my mind's not exactly buzzing. All I can think of at the moment is to steer clear of both of them for the time being, don't let yourself get pushed into a corner. If you can get some leave, come up and stay with me for a week or so.'

Veronica groaned. 'If only I could, but I'm not due holidays yet. As for keeping out of their way, I've already invited them both to dinner tonight. Neither knows that the other is coming—I thought a confrontation might clear the air.'

There was silence for some seconds, then Liz said, 'You're a brave woman, Vee. Let me know how it goes.'

Veronica put her head in her hands and groaned when she finished the call. 'Stupid, not brave,' she muttered. Dear God, what had she done? She was dreading tonight.

* * *

But the dinner party never happened.

There was a rail crash a few miles outside the city and all hospitals on special alert swung into action. Two full commuter trains were in a headlong collision and there were an unknown number of casualties.

At seven-thirty, when Veronica, Jeremy and Alec should have been standing sipping sherry in her sitting room and wondering what to say to each other, they were all three sweating away in the resuscitation rooms of A and E.

This was almost foreign territory for Jeremy, who was normally only called there in his specialist capacity, not doing general first-aid surgery as he was now. But rehearsals of who should go where in the event of an all-hospitals alert directed that he, together with any other specialists who were free, should make himself available to work where needed.

As always in an acute emergency, there was a flood of volunteers—with both doctors and nurses and auxiliary staff who were off duty coming in as soon as they heard the news or were contacted by the personnel department.

A and E were first on the list to be offered help as they were in the direct line of fire. Alec, with his flair for organisation, and with Veronica to help him, made quick assessments and chose his emergency staff intelligently, distributing them about the department where he considered them most suited.

Some he sent to act as triage officers, to sort out grades of injury, not a job to be envied. It was a difficult task, determining who was most in need of expert help, even following Alec's rules of breathing, bleeding, broken bones, babies, because there were so many victims involved.

He sent a paediatric physician to sort out the babies and

children, and Veronica supplied a nurse with paediatric experience to assist him. Other doctors and nurses were detailed to work in the cubicles, with a regular A and E medic in a supervisory role. Some patients with minor injuries were being treated in a screened-off area in Reception, which was steadily filling up with more crash victims and police officers and anxious relatives.

The first victims began to be admitted at five-thirty—four hours ago. Alec had asked Veronica to work with Jeremy, one of the few surgeons he had chosen to work in Resus.

'No point in putting square pegs in round holes,' he'd remarked curtly to Veronica at the beginning of the evening. 'Not all surgeons can work competently and at speed.'

So Jeremy was one of only three of the volunteer surgeons who were allowed to work in Alec's holy of holies. Alec's face had brightened when one of them, Monica Maybridge, on the point of retirement, her short grey hair flying all over the place, had shown up, puffing rather because she was a bit overweight and had been hurrying.

'Barring me,' he'd said, 'Monica's the best general surgeon in the hospital to wield a scalpel.'

As far as possible, assisted by Diana Ferguson and a team of nurses, Monica worked on the children. She was a wizard with them, and the ones who were conscious responded to her in an extraordinary fashion.

Alec worked with a senior house officer and a young man still doing his rotation but who had impressed Alec when he had worked in A and E a few months before.

With Dick Shepherd and Janice and other experienced staff away with the field team attending the accident site, Veronica and Jeremy were left to work together with occasional assistance from Teddy Smith, the most senior house officer. Teddy was spreading himself around, keeping an eye on what was happening in Reception.

Jeremy said softly, carefully removing some obvious shards of glass and metal from the abdomen of a middle-aged lady loaded with analgesics, which had a sedative effect, 'I daren't do more—might set off a bleed. The rest will have to be done in Theatre.' He bent over the patient and stroked back her hair from her dirt-smudged forehead.

They didn't know her name and Veronica thought that this was one of the worst features of this sort of accident—no name made you almost a non-person.

Jeremy noted the woman's wedding ring and continued gently, 'Mrs... can you hear me?' No response. 'You are in the casualty unit of the Porthampton University Hospital. You've been involved in a train accident and we're going to send you up to a special ward for treatment and an operation.'

Hospital rules made it necessary to explain what was going on even when the patient appeared to be unconscious. Everyone agreed that it was a good rule, and one which occasionally triggered off a response. Their comatose patient didn't respond, though, and as soon as they'd finished tidying her wound she was sent up to the trauma unit.

The stream of victims seemed never-ending and many of them had similar injuries, which often happened where numbers of people were involved. Experienced doctors like Alec could tell after a couple of casualties had been dealt with what the bulk of injuries would be.

Apparently the lady with abdominal injuries wasn't typical, they learned from Steve and Tess, the paramedics who'd brought her in. They thought that she might have been trying to climb out of a window over shattered glass and metal.

Many of the injuries were broken bones, particularly arms and legs, consistent with being thrown forward as the carriages collided. There were also quite a few facial injuries, broken noses and jaws and cheekbones, caused by the victims being propelled forward and hitting the floor or another hard surface violently.

Veronica said softly when she and Jeremy were patching up someone's face, 'I guess you'll be much in demand over the next few weeks, doing all these repair jobs.'

Jeremy delicately placed an antiseptic gauze dressing over the split and broken nose of a young woman who was asthmatic. Her nose was bleeding profusely, and Veronica secured the dressing with a type of adhesive tape which could be easily removed.

It had been decided to lightly anaesthetise the young woman by injection as she was understandably agitated by her injury, which could only make her breathing difficulties worse for some time to come.

While they were waiting for her to be taken up to Trauma, Veronica held an oxygen mask a few inches away from the bloody nose to help her breathing as she came round.

It was a moment before Jeremy replied to Veronica's remark about facial repairs. 'Too right. It's going to be a hell of a job fitting them all in—my list is top-heavy as it is.' He looked up and caught Veronica's eye. 'But not too busy to see you, love, ever, remember that.'

She caught her breath. How on earth could he think of that amidst all these injured people? *Because he loves you, truly loves you,* murmured her private voice in the back of her head.

At some time late in the evening the field team came back. Janice reported to Veronica when there was a brief lull in the resuscitation room and Jeremy had gone out to look at some of the patients waiting to be seen by him or Alec or Monica. The cardiac crash team, directed by registrar Bob Standish, had been busy all evening in the screened-off area at the end of Resus, and they were still busy as patients in heart failure continued to be brought in.

'It was absolute carnage out there,' said Janice sounding and looking grim, grubby and weary. 'But the organisation was good. We ran out of everything a while ago—plasma, anti-tetanus, general fluids, etc.—and were told that we could leave as teams from more distant hospitals had arrived. So, now I'm here, what do you want me to do?'

'Go home,' replied Veronica firmly. 'We'll all be going off at midnight. Management have got their act together and we're to be relieved in an hour or so. A whole new team is taking over for the rest of the night, along with some of the regulars who are already here. Even Alec's agreed to it. I've never seen him look so tired and grey. We're all tired, but on him it really shows.'

'His age, I suppose, but I bet he said something about wanting us in bright and early tomorrow.' Janice grinned a tired grin.

'You're a mind-reader,' said Veronica dryly.

'I know the boss,' said Janice, and with a wave wafted herself out of the room.

As soon as she was relieved by the night sister, Veronica seized her coat and bag and rushed out of a side door to avoid the handful of reporters at the front entrance. She was desperate to get away before either Jeremy or Alec waylaid her. She couldn't face them.

They had been so busy all evening and she had been so focused on her patients that she hadn't given the aborted dinner party a thought, but now the pressure was off, exhausted as she was, it came back to haunt her. What on earth had she hoped to achieve by it?

'Sorry about that,' she confessed to no one in particular as she unlocked her car. 'Tomorrow I shall come clean and tell them what I'd meant to do. They'll probably both go off me then.' Which was, she knew, a positive lie. Neither of them would back off—Jeremy because he was in love with her, and Alec because he considered her his protégé with whom he'd formed a great rapport.

Veronica set her alarm for the usual time of six-thirty, and woke just before it went off. She'd given mid-morning starts to many of her regular staff who had worked late, but she'd asked Janice and a couple of other seniors to come in at the usual time. She simply didn't have the staff to cover them.

All the theatre lights were still blazing, she noticed as she drew up in the car park, and had been going all night, she guessed.

She wasn't in the least surprised to see Jeremy waiting for her at the staff entrance, leaning against the wall beside the door. He looked immaculate in a dark pinstripe suit and dazzling white shirt. No one would have guessed that he had worked hours in A and E as well as in his own theatre. Remembering Janice's remark last night, she presumed it was the age difference between Jeremy and Alec that made the one look bright and alert, whilst the older one looked dead beat—well, he had last night.

'Morning,' said Jeremy cheerfully, bending to kiss her cheek, uncaring of the fact that staff were coming and going through the automatic doors. 'Love you,' he murmured, taking her bag containing a clean uniform from her unresisting hand and leading the way toward her office. 'How long will hand-over take?' he asked, and kissed her again on her other cheek.

Veronica gathered herself together as she hurried after him. 'Quite a while,' she murmured breathily. 'There was still a lot going on when we left. We've got drugs and things to sort out—every last needle has to be accounted for.'

'I still love you,' he said, seeming to ignore what she was saying.

This is a crazy conversation to be having, she thought, nodding and smiling at other staff as they passed, giving them curious looks. The looks, she noted, were mainly directed at Jeremy.

'Will you be through by ten?'

'Have to be. We'll be open for business as usual by then and I'll be out on the prowl.'

They reached her door. Jeremy plonked her bag down beside the door. 'Let's meet for coffee at ten, my office. It's more of a sanctum than yours is, we can depend on a little peace and quiet.'

She opened her mouth to protest, but he put his finger over her lips, 'Ten o'clock,' he said.

Her mind going like the clappers, she raced through what work she could. The mound of paperwork generated by yesterday's emergency would have to be tackled later, but she fulfilled one obligation that she had determined to do and sought out all the staff who had worked so hard yesterday to thank them personally.

The last person on her list was Rebecca, who had somehow kept some sort of order in Reception and had stayed until midnight, filling in details of patient's names and addresses and gathering information from the police when victims themselves couldn't talk.

She'd also made sure that the coffee and drinks machine had been tanked up to supply relatives and the paramedics who'd dashed in and out and had been easy to overlook.

It was coming up to ten o'clock as Veronica finished thanking Rebecca for her marathon effort.

Rebecca dismissed her thanks. 'I couldn't do what you lot were doing in Resus, saving lives. Too much blood.' She shuddered. 'And the boss was marvellous. I've always admired him as a doctor, but not as a man until last night. The way he kept everyone together… And when he popped out occasionally into Reception, he made a beeline for the kids who were waiting to be seen and actually made some of them laugh. And he gave me the thumbs-up sign when he left—amazing.' She grinned. 'I'm his slave for life.'

Veronica grinned, too. 'That'll make his day,' she said, and waved goodbye.

But once out of Reception she leaned against the wall for a moment and closed her eyes. But we didn't save them all, she thought bleakly.

Sharp on ten o'clock, she tapped and entered Jeremy's office, not waiting for him to invite her. If she waited, she might run away. He came to greet her, his arms outstretched as if they hadn't seen each other for a long time.

Veronica licked her lips, which were suddenly dry, and, trying to control the croak in her voice, pointed that out as he took her hands and drew her to him.

'But it is a long time,' he said ruefully. 'Hours. Tell me honestly, my love, hasn't it dragged for you, too?'

*Honestly!* Yes, it had dragged in spite of being busy. She couldn't wait to see him. It was exciting and unnerving, too. But should she tell him that? She mustn't let herself be diverted from the two things that she had to say to him. So she ignored his plea, pulled her hands from his and pointed to the slip of a room that served as his cloakroom and a miniature kitchen.

'Please, coffee first.' Her voice was stronger with hardly a crack in it.

Jeremy pushed her gently into the comfortable chair that faced his desk. 'Coffee on the way.'

It was hot and strong and sweet, but before she could protest he stopped her. 'I know that you don't like sugar, but you need it, and by the look in your eyes and the set of that determined chin, I think that I'm going to need it, too.'

Was she really that transparent? Veronica took a slug of coffee and almost choked, but waved Jeremy away when he made to rub her back.

'Not necessary,' she croaked out.

He went round the desk and sat in his usual place, but his mouth looked stern, his dark eyes unreadable. 'I think you'd better get on with it,' he said, 'before you lose your nerve or burst.'

She tried a smile. 'What, and mess up your beautiful carpet?'

It didn't work. His expression didn't alter. He looked grim and forbidding and glanced at his watch. 'I allowed half an hour for us to talk,' he said from somewhere deep in his throat, 'about us and our relationship. We've spent nearly ten minutes frittering away the time. If you've something to say, Veronica, please, say it or let me talk.' His voice was icy, so changed from their early morning meeting or when he'd greeted her when she'd arrived.

She looked at him in surprise and dismay. She hadn't expected this coolness, had, in fact, banked on his gentleness, his *love* for her. There was very little love in his voice right now, and suddenly she realised why—he was as nervous as she. His competent, steady hands were clasping his coffee-mug until the knuckles showed white.

'I don't know why you're so angry and nervous,' she said. 'I'm the one who has a confession to make and I'm certainly not looking forward to it.'

'A confession? What on earth have you got to confess? I'm the one with a whole lot of baggage of guilt from the past that I long to expiate.' The icy coldness had gone out of his voice, replaced with obvious relief. What had he thought she was going to say?

She said bluntly, 'You've nothing to expiate if you're referring to the Greek episode. As to my confession, I planned to bring you and Alec face to face over dinner last night, an unpleasant, spiteful thing to do.'

'Oh, that.' He waved it aside. 'I thought that's what you were up to and I guess Alec did, too. Do you mean to say that was all it was? As for being spiteful, you haven't a spiteful bone in your body. I presume that you thought that it might help.'

'Oh! So I've been getting het-up for nothing.'

He grinned and swallowed the last of his coffee. 'Now, my turn to talk.'

'*No!* I've something else to say.' Very quickly, before she really lost it, she gabbled, 'I want you to examine my scar and operate on it if you think you can do anything about it.'

Jeremy's face was a picture as it went through various phases—disbelief, amazement, delight. He slammed his mug down and moved swiftly round the desk, pulling her out of the chair and holding her close.

Veronica put up a show of fighting him off but, in fact, the last thing she wanted was for him to let go of her. She was safe in his arms.

'What made you change your mind?' he asked hoarsely.

'You, telling me to get a life for myself, the carnage we saw yesterday, and what you said about having a second chance. There were too many people yesterday who won't have a second chance at putting things right because they're too traumatised physically or emotionally—or they're dead. It seemed churlish and ungrateful not to put right something that might be righted, just because—' She put her hand over her mouth to stop further words rushing out.

'Because of our changed roles, and you still not quite being able to come to terms with the fact that the youth who came from the wrong side of the tracks, as our American cousins say, has pulled himself up by his bootstraps, and is quite respectable these days?'

She was doubly glad that he was holding her, or she would surely have collapsed in a heap at his feet. And it was a bonus to be able to hide her face against his chest. Her cheeks were a fiery red—he must despise her. She despised herself, and made herself look up into his hooded eyes.

'Oh, Jeremy, I'm so sorry, so very sorry. The last thing that I want to do is to hurt you…'

'Hush!' His voice was soft and whispery. He kissed her gently on the mouth, and then the forehead, and half carried her back to the chair. He sat her down and placed his hands on the arms of the chair.

'You haven't hurt me, love. Your feelings aren't so different to what mine were when I suddenly realised who it was that Alec wanted me to see. Reverse snobbery reared its ugly head, and for a few moments I positively relished the idea that I had something to offer you, the snooty little rich girl who had laughed at my spots.'

'You never showed how you felt. You were kind and understanding from the moment I woke up on that lovely sun-warmed bench in the square and found you looking at me. It was like something out of a book—Her Past Catches up with Her. I could only think of how badly I'd behaved, and felt so ashamed.' She added sadly, 'And, you see, even then I could only think about myself, when I should have been rejoicing for you, for your achievements, and having overcome our problem.'

Jeremy straightened up. 'That's not quite true,' he said, pointing to his cleft chin. 'Even the best plastic surgery couldn't do anything about this, the damage was too deep, but I am fortunate that it's disguised itself as what has been described as a fascinating dimple.' His mouth tilted into a wicked smile. 'The ladies love it.'

Veronica stared at the dimple, then tentatively touched it with a forefinger. 'I think I love it, too,' she whispered.

What would have happened next, she wondered, later in the day, if his secretary hadn't come in to remind him that he had an outpatients clinic? He had thanked Maude with his usual courtesy and had asked her to let his registrar know that he would be down shortly and to make a start without him. 'And please bring me the appointments book, Maude.'

Maude's eyes had flickered to Veronica and back to Jeremy. 'You've nothing free for weeks,' she'd said.

Jeremy had nodded. 'Nevertheless…' he smiled '…I'll have the book, please.'

Maude nodded. 'I'll fetch it,' she'd said, and had given Veronica a nice smile as she'd gone out.

She and Jeremy didn't touch after that, but tender vibes passed between them, so fragile that they didn't dare speak, just looked hungrily at each other. Each was so totally aware of the other, and only the other, that Maude tapped and entered and placed the appointments book in Jeremy's hand without either of them noticing.

Something incredible had happened. After endless minutes, Jeremy closed the book with a snap and muttered hoarsely, 'We'll sort this out tonight over dinner. Oh, dear love, I'm just so, so pleased, happy, ecstatic. You are sure about this? It might not work, you know.'

'So you said before. But I have absolute faith in you, Jeremy. If anyone can do it, you can, and if it doesn't work, I'll be no worse off than I have been for years. I've never felt so sure of anything in my life.' Veronica's eyes were shining, her cheeks faintly flushed, and two or three wisps of red-gold hair had escaped from the combs.

He touched her then, to take out the combs and reposition them, tucking in the stray wisps. 'You'll wear it loose tonight with long dangly earrings, won't you? Not to cover your scar, but because it's gorgeous and sends my blood pressure sky high. It's like a shiny, rippling curtain and takes me back to *A Midsummer Night's Dream*, only now I'm in with a chance, which I wasn't then.'

'If that's what you want, I shall wear it that way.'

'It is. There was a film star in the forties. My mum was—is—an addict of old films. Her name was Veronica Lake, another Veronica, you see. That was how she wore her hair.' Jeremy's mouth softened.

'Did you fancy her?'

'Dear love, I fancied every female, alive or on film, since they were totally beyond my grasp. But, yes, she was special. My sort of girl, I thought when I was about twelve and saw her for the first time. A girl called Veronica with strawberry blonde hair, that's the sort of girl I want to marry.'

'And that's the sort of girl you've got,' said Veronica softly.

'And even if the scar repair doesn't work out? Will you still consider marrying me?'

She hesitated. 'Yes, I'm almost sure that I will.'

'Only almost?'

'I made a vow when this happened that I wouldn't marry or enter into a long-term relationship that would expose me to my partner before I was able to put on my disguise in the morning. I know that I'm prepared to break that vow for you, but it won't be easy, I shall need time. Breaking a vow, even a whacky one, as my friend, Liz, describes it, is difficult.' She laid a hand on his arm. 'Does that make sense?'

'Perfect sense,' he said. 'For people like you and me, sometimes it's the only thing that one can do to overcome the trauma of pain and disfigurement. When my acne first started to respond to treatment, I was terrified of making dates, and then went mad and really played the field.'

He frowned. 'I must have hurt some young women, not realising that they were taking me seriously. I vowed then that any relationships I formed, however brief, would be outside the hospital unless, and until, the right woman came along...and she has. So I do understand about your vow, and I'll be as patient as I can be.'

'You're good on patience,' she whispered. 'That's all I needed to know.'

## CHAPTER NINE

AS SMARTLY on time as ever, Jeremy arrived at Heatherington House to collect her at seven-thirty. Veronica, waiting impatiently by the window, saw him arrive and hurried down the stairs to meet him.

'What, no coffee before we go?' he teased, leaning over to open the passenger door for her.

She climbed up into the Range Rover, showing a lot of silk-stockinged leg through the slit in her simple satin Chinese tunic that went so well with her hairstyle.

'Mmm, like it.' His voice was admiring, appreciative. He touched the long silver earrings that shimmered in the evening sunlight.

Veronica shrugged. 'The dressing up is for you,' she said quickly, throwing in a tiny smile, 'because you requested it. It's not that I wanted to dress up, I just want to get on with this discussion about this...' She pulled aside the curtain of hair and revealed the puckered half-moon scar framing her left eye, clearly visible without make-up.

Jeremy stared at her for a moment and muttered, 'Oh, my love.' Then he put the car into gear.

'That sounds ominous,' Veronica said tautly. 'Is it worse than you thought?'

He shook his head. 'No, but you're expecting too much too soon. We are nowhere near the point of where we can consider surgery. There's a lot of talking to do yet.'

They were driving along the open road on top of the downs. The view was spectacular—they could see right along the coast to the east with its steep white cliffs in the distance and right below them the silver pier marching out into the sea. The air was like wine.

But Veronica was hardly aware of either. The tone of his voice frightened her. Was Jeremy drawing back from his offer, regretting it? Her stomach dropped like a stone. Now that she had scraped up the courage to get something done, was it all going to come to nothing?

Smoothly he lifted one hand from the wheel and wrapped it warmly round her cold, clenched fists. 'I'm not going to tell you to relax, because I know that you would if you could. But I'm going to suggest that you think about this rationally.'

'Rationally,' repeated Veronica dully. 'This could be the most exciting moment of my life, and you want me to treat it rationally, and I thought…'

'That because we are friends—more than friends, I hope—and colleagues and I said that I would treat you any time, it meant that treatment would be rushed through.'

The first bristling of anger prickled through her. She pulled her hands from beneath his palm. 'Yes, that's what I thought. It's what you implied.' She turned a stony face to stare at his profile. 'I'm beginning to think that you just used this scar to promote your marriage plans.' She watched his face grow grimmer and felt a frisson of fear as he pulled off the road onto the grass verge and stopped.

He released his seat belt, turned and released hers, then took hold of her shoulders and twisted her to face him. His hands hurt and she winced, but he didn't release his grip. 'Don't you *ever*,' he gritted, 'accuse me of using my professional expertise to further my own ends.' He was white to his taut lips, the hurt showed in his blue-black eyes.

Against the pressure of his hands imprisoning her shoulders, Veronica brought her palms up to her face and covered it. She could feel hot tears seeping between her fingers and tried to dash them away. She rarely cried, had never burst into tears since she'd been an adult, but she felt like doing that at this moment. The full import of what she had said to him hit her. How could she have hurt him so badly, this man with an unblemished record for dedication, even from those who didn't like him?

'I'm sorry, I'm sorry,' she whispered. 'I don't know why I said those dreadful things. I didn't mean them, I didn't mean to hurt you.'

Jeremy eased her hands from her face and kissed her wet palms. His rage had left him as suddenly as it had manifested itself.

He said in a soft voice, 'Of course you didn't, my love. You keyed yourself up for something to happen, and when it didn't you felt like a pricked balloon and desperately disappointed and wanted to hit out at something or someone. You've had too much excitement for one day, and that means tears before bedtime.'

Veronica sniffed and tugged her hands from his. 'You're full of these old-fashioned proverbs,' she muttered. She fumbled for a handkerchief, a scrap of fine cotton with lace edging.

Jeremy gave a little snort of derision. 'That won't get you far,' he said. 'Look in the glove compartment, there are tissues there.'

Sniffing as she opened the compartment and grabbed a handful of tissues, Veronica felt the tension seeping away and suddenly burst out laughing. Perhaps it was a little hysterical, but at least she was laughing. 'At this point,' she snuffled, blowing her nose vigorously, 'you are supposed to hand me a large, crisp white handkerchief for me to weep into.'

'A la the best romantic literature.' He chuckled. 'Sorry, I missed out on that bit of foreplay. I only get to read women's mags when I go to the dentist. I'll read anything there to keep my mind off the coming ordeal.'

Veronica opened her eyes wide. 'Are you scared of going to the dentist?' she asked in astonishment.

He nodded. 'You bet. Why—aren't you? I thought everyone hated going to the dentist.'

'No, an uncle of mine is a professor of dentistry and I've been seeing him since before I can remember.'

'It follows. You always had beautiful teeth, so white and perfect. Have you ever had a filling?'

'No—have you?'

'Dozens. My teeth were nearly as troublesome as my acne at one time. My mum and I practically lived at the dentist's surgery for some years. She was wonderful. Don't know how she managed it, fitting in that, rarely missing a school event and going out to work.'

There was a lot she would like to know about his mum, but she felt that now wasn't the time to ask. 'They're lovely now, your teeth,' she said instead.

'Lots of expensive dental work.'

She frowned and abruptly moved away from him, struggling to find the end of her seat belt. 'I don't know what we're doing, sitting here talking about teeth,' she muttered grumpily, 'unless you're trying to distract me. Don't you think it's time we went? I'm starving.'

'Good,' he said, putting the car in gear. 'Let's go.'

Jeremy's house at the end of a long winding drive, an old sixteenth-century farmhouse, was a surprise. They passed a cottage at the foot of the drive and he nodded toward it. 'Poll and Greg live there—they look after the house and the farm. Capable pair. I couldn't manage without them.'

'Oh, sort of old retainers,' Veronica commented.

Jeremy laughed. 'Hardly. Greg was in the army and was injured in a peace-keeping mission somewhere that was anything but peaceful, but he grew up on a farm and wanted to get back to it. He's thirty-something. He had facial wounds and I patched him up. He needed a job and I needed someone to manage the estate. It's worked out fine.'

'And Poll?'

'She's also thirty-something. She can turn her hand to anything, a modern professional woman with a mixed portfolio. She cooks, helps on the farm, keeps the accounts, can surf the internet faster than anyone I've seen. She's one of those truly all-round women who seem to pop up these days… She's, well, a manager and a damn good one. You'll like her, and Greg, too.'

'I imagined,' said Veronica, gazing up at the black and white front and casement windows when she got out of the car, 'that you lived in a smart service flat, a real bachelor pad. You sounded like a flat person when you told me once that you had no one to put lemon and ice into your drink, yet here you are, being waited on hand and foot by a pair of perfect paragons.'

He shuddered. 'A service flat. No, thanks, I had enough of living in flats when I was a kid. The constant noise, graffiti, filthy lifts that rarely worked. Being a bit scared much of the time because I didn't belong to a gang.' He straightened his shoulders and the muscles bulged slightly beneath the rolled-up sleeves of his blue and white striped shirt.

The shirt was unbuttoned at the top, revealing a V of

tanned chest and a scattering of dark hairs. There was a small cluster at his throat beneath his Adam's apple, fanning out lower down to be hidden by the rest of the buttoned-up shirt.

Veronica turned away abruptly. Jeremy oozed sexiness, made more potent because he seemed unaware of it. No wonder he hid under a cloak of indifference to women. He certainly wouldn't get a moment's peace if he made himself available.

There were rustlings and chirpings and small darting movements of birds overhead. She looked up.

'House martins,' he said. 'Under the eaves. They come every year.' He cupped her face with both hands and kissed her. 'I'm so glad that you're here. I've so wanted you to see my home.' He placed a hand beneath her elbow and, ignoring the heavy oak door, steered her toward a side door.

'Thought we'd eat in the kitchen,' he said, 'rather than traipse through to the dining room. Besides, it's sunnier, faces west and catches the evening sun.'

The sunlight burst on them as they exited from the long dark corridor and stepped into a farmhouse kitchen fit to grace the pages of *Homes and Gardens*—and yet it looked lived in, even slightly shabby, but in an arty sort of way. An old refectory table, lined by Windsor armchairs, was set for two, a bowl of pansies glowed mutedly in the middle of the table. An old sofa in the window embrasure at the far end begged to be sat upon. A cheerful red Aga emitted aromatic scents. Saucepans, dishes and kitchen utensils were lined up on the walls between ancient black beams.

'This is the oldest part of the house.' Jeremy took her arm and led her down the length of the kitchen to the sofa. 'Said to be left over from the wattle-and-daub part of the original building. Now, sit down and let's have a civilised drink. Dry vermouth, isn't it?'

Struck dumb by the quiet sumptuousness of it all, Veronica nodded. Used to creature comforts all her life, she was still overawed by the feeling of old money that had been at work here for generations. So how had Jeremy acquired a home like this? He'd only been a consultant for a short while and registrars didn't make the sort of money to afford something like this, even if they wrote learned theses and gave lectures.

He read her mind as he sometimes seemed able to do. 'A distinguished old gentleman left all this to me in his will,' he said. 'An extravagant way of saying thank you for doing a successful emergency repair on his wife's face when she was involved in an RTA. That was some years ago when I was still a registrar. She died a year later of cancer, and he died not long after that, though I knew nothing of this as I had no contact with them.'

Veronica said softly, 'Your distinguished old gentleman must have loved his wife very much to make such a generous gift in her memory. Didn't anyone dispute the will?'

Jeremy shook his head. 'No, apparently neither of the old people had family, and there was no legal reason for not accepting since the old man had never been my patient. The will wasn't contested...except by me.'

'You!' said Veronica, startled.

'Yes. It didn't feel right somehow, accepting such a magnificent gift from someone I'd hardly known, and could barely remember. I was only doing my job. His wife was one of many patients I treated in that accident. She was only in for a short while, and had follow-up treatment in Outpatients. But her husband learned that it was having immediate expert attention that saved her from being badly scarred, hence the gratitude.'

Veronica met Jeremy's eyes. 'I can understand that. I'd have given anything to have had you around when this happened.' With a quick gesture she touched her scar.

She wished that she hadn't when she saw the flicker of hurt in Jeremy's eyes. She had forgotten for a moment that he still blamed himself for not staying with her after the earthquake.

'So what made you change your mind about accepting this lovely old house, Jeremy?' she said quickly.

Jeremy strolled to the window and then back again and stood in front of her, rocking on the balls of his feet.

'My solicitor pointed out that if I refused it, it would go to the exchequer. If I accepted, I could do with it what I wanted once it was mine—sell it, or give it away. He urged me to accept and give some thought about what to do with it.'

'And have you?'

He nodded and drained his glass of wine. 'The council have just agreed plans for me to build a couple of bungalows where patients can come to convalesce after leaving hospital, a stepping-stone to home. There'll be a warden with nursing experience to supervise. If it's successful, I hope to extend it—there's plenty of ground over the other side of the estate.'

Veronica's eyes were shining. 'What a brilliant idea, Jeremy. So many people are discharged home too soon to free beds when they're not really ready. I'm sure that your old gentleman would have appreciated your plans. Perhaps when building gets under way, you'll keep me in the picture regarding progress.'

'I shall do better than that—you'll be able to make an inspection from time to time. Now, can I get you another drink?'

Veronica drained her glass and shook her head. 'I'd

rather eat,' she said. 'And then talk about this.' She indicated her scar again. 'Or is it forbidden?'

'Of course not.' Jeremy pulled her up from the sofa and gave her a quick, warm kiss. 'After we've eaten, we'll start what is virtually the beginning of your treatment.'

They fed on watercress soup, tender chicken casserole and, astonishingly, an old-fashioned rice pudding with a crisp nutmeg brown skin over the top.

'What is it?' Veronica asked and sniffed. 'It smells nice.'

He raised his eyebrows. 'Haven't you ever eaten rice pudding before? It was a great standby when I was a kid. Mum used to put one in the oven on a low gas, so that by the time we got home in the evening it would be just about right.'

'Rice pudding! But it's not like the hospital rice pudding, and I don't recall ever having rice as a pudding at home. I have the hospital pudding occasionally when I'm really hungry, but it doesn't smell like this.'

'Believe me, it doesn't taste like it either.' Jeremy laughed. 'Poll likes to surprise people. She's perfectly capable of producing a modern meal, low-fat, low-calorie everything, decorative rather than nourishing, but as she says in her Scottish accent, "You won't get very braw on that."'

Veronica wasn't sure if 'braw' was what she wanted to be, but she finished her pudding down to the last spoonful and sighed with pleasure. 'I must ask Poll for the recipe.'

He nodded approval. 'I'm sure she'd be pleased to pass it on to you. Now, I think we should take our coffee through to my study—well, it's more of a workroom really—and start talking shop.'

Almost imperceptibly Jeremy's manner changed when they reached his study, which was rather like his office at the hospital only more leathery and comfortable and lived-in—and larger. The walls were crammed from floor to ceiling with books—dozens of medical texts which were to be expected, but also shelves full of detective and science-fiction novels, and a smattering of poetry.

In addition to a handsome walnut desk, there was a long table with some large, heavy books and a notepad on it, a realistic model head in two halves showing nerve and blood vessel endings, and a futuristic-looking monitor and box of tricks at the other end of the table, where presumably Poll surfed the net.

Lucky Poll, thought Veronica wryly, to be so well thought of by the boss.

Easily slipping into the role of doctor, Jeremy began without preamble as they sat down.

'When you are considering plastic surgery, you have to prepare yourself for what is going to be a long haul. It's not something to take on lightly, Veronica. Is there someone you could discuss this with—your family, a friend?'

Veronica looked bewildered. 'But I thought that I was going to discuss it with you.'

'That's what we are going to do, but I was thinking of someone on a more personal level, I've got to look at it from the professional angle. Certainly you and I have to establish a rapport as doctor and patient, but it's good to have a lay person's input, too. I wouldn't like you, love, to think that I'd over-persuaded or under-persuaded you about treatment, especially if it doesn't work.'

'I would never do that. I trust you implicitly.'

Jeremy sipped his coffee and looked at her over the rim of the cup, his dark eyes lovingly searching her face. 'Right now you do,' he said, 'but, believe me, after a few sessions you may begin to have doubts. You'll need to talk to someone who has your interests at heart. Trust me,

Veronica, I know what I'm talking about. You'll begin to be frustrated and wonder why active treatment hasn't begun. You'll start imagining things, wondering if I am holding something back that I don't want you to know.'

She shook her had. 'I'll never believe that.'

'You must think of yourself as having been suffering from a chronic disease for a long time, with its associated trauma of coming to terms with second best—a condition like that takes a hell of a lot of getting over. It's like someone trying to learn to walk again after a stroke or severe injury—you wouldn't expect a patient to run before he walks. It takes the physio and sometimes a counsellor, as well as doctors and nurses, to help the process.'

He stood up and went to a cupboard and returned with a bottle and two glasses. 'Brandy,' he said. 'A very good one. Sip it slowly. It'll warm you and help you to sleep...'

'But—'

'No buts, we've talked enough.' He dropped a kiss on her head. 'I'll give you some leaflets to study and I want you to make a note of any questions you may want answered next time we meet, officially or semi-officially.'

He said nothing about meeting socially, Veronica thought bleakly. Did this mean that at least temporarily he wanted to put distance between them? The thought filled her with dread. It had dawned on her at last that life would be empty without him.

They met a few days later. Alec had called Jeremy in to check a patient who had been involved in an accident and received facial injuries. Veronica, her heart fluttering uncomfortably at Jeremy's proximity, stood back and watched the two of them standing side by side as they examined the patient in great detail. These two supposedly hard men who weren't hard at all.

Alec looked small beside Jeremy, small and diminished. She felt guilty. She and Alec had said very little to each other over the last few days, but when she met his eyes there was an expression in their brown depths that told her that he considered her his protégé.

The two men moved away from the couch, leaving her to finish cleaning and lightly dressing the wounds and reasssuring the patient.

Alec's bleeper went off and he went to a phone.

Jeremy waited by the cubicle curtains until she'd finished dealing with the patient, then held the curtain aside and followed her out. 'Meet you at the side door? A working lunch at our beach at one?' he said softly. 'I'll bring the food.'

The combination of 'working' and 'our beach' seemed odd. She took a deep breath. 'All right,' she murmured, 'a working lunch.'

A and E was busy for the rest of the morning, but it was the sort of business that they were used to and could cope with. Veronica took herself to her office and began the never-ending job of catching up with paperwork.

She was ready to go off just before one, but was delayed by a phone call. By the time she left the office it was ten past one. She hurried along the corridor and ran into Alec. 'Late for a lunch date?' he asked smoothly.

'A working lunch,' she replied briskly.

His eyes gleamed. 'Ah, you've started treatment—good.'

'How do you know that, Alec?'

'I know Jeremy's methods, very sound. Listen to him, Veronica.' Lifting his hand in salute, he walked off.

The beach was as warm and isolated as it had been on their first visit. Jeremy laid out the picnic he'd brought—

not canteen sandwiches but home-made smoked salmon ones, a ham and mushroom quiche and a bunch of black seedless grapes. He poured chilled fruit juice from a cool flask and kissed her at the same time. 'You look tired,' he said.

'I haven't been sleeping well,' she faltered.

'Why?' He cut a slice of quiche and handed it to her on a plate with a fork.

'Because, having read the literature you gave me, I'm very aware of the trickiness of the surgery you'll have to do. And—and the possibility that it won't work, and that there's even an outside chance it might make matters worse.'

'Not a high risk,' Jeremy said. 'That's why I gave you a breakdown of my personal success rates to compare with other surgeons', not to boast about but to reassure. I show them to all my patients—how else are they to judge my expertise? Why should they trust me with their bodies when maybe there's a better surgeon down the road?'

'But doesn't it frighten a lot of people off?'

'Generally, no. The intelligent ones question it, as you're doing, the others seem to be reassured by my success rate, and GPs welcome it. Most of them are as ignorant of the statistics as their patients. In fact, there have been stirrings for some time for there to be a league table of experts all over the country, not only in the plastics field but covering all surgery.'

He took a large bite out of a sandwich. 'After all, we shop around to get the best that we can afford when we're buying a car or a pair of shoes, so why not shop around for the best surgeon to operate on your body? But you can only make comparisons if you've got the facts.'

Veronica frowned. 'Well, it's easy in your case—you've got an international reputation and are the youngest consultant in the business and I work with you—but I don't know of any other plastic surgeons except those in your team.'

'Then do as I suggest in my notes—get in touch with the appropriate association of plastic surgeons and ask their advice.'

An expression of disbelief spread over her lovely face and her mouth trembled. 'Are you saying,' she whispered, 'that you would rather I saw somebody else?'

He gathered her in his arms and showered her with kisses. She breathed the familiar scent of him in deeply. 'Oh, my dear, lovely Veronica, of course not.' His voice was a deep, throaty, rumble that vibrated in his broad chest. It was very comforting beneath her ear. 'I wouldn't normally operate on someone so close to me, but the trust has given me permission because they consider that I'm the right chap for the job.'

He looked thoughtful, and added, 'And that was mainly on account of Alec's support. But I want you to feel free to shop around if you want to.'

Veronica was surprised. 'Do you mean that you had to ask the trust's permission to operate on me?'

'Yes. There were one or two people who thought that there might be questions asked, since it is known that we are old friends and have a current relationship. An old rule of medicine, of course, that one shouldn't operate on one's nearest and dearest. Reasonable enough, generally speaking, but they decided not to apply it in this case.'

'That's big of them,' said Veronica sarcastically, 'because I wouldn't let anyone else touch me.' She lifted her head and looked him in the eye. 'I only want the best, Jeremy. I don't need to shop around,' she announced firmly. 'I want you. Thanks for being so patient with me and explaining. I'm beginning to understand what you mean by building up a relationship of trust.'

Feeling resolute and strong, she stood up and brushed the crumbs from her uniform skirt and began gathering up the picnic remains. She smiled down at Jeremy, sitting with his head bent, juggling a few pebbles from one hand to the other. The sun shone on his thick black hair. Oh, I do love him, she thought with a rush of tenderness.

'Come on,' she said, her voice brisk to hide her emotion. 'Let's get cracking, we have jobs to go to.'

## CHAPTER TEN

MUZZY from her pre-med, Veronica watched the ceiling lights flicker overhead as she was wheeled from the side ward to Theatre on a trolley. It was a weird sensation, as if she were detached from her surroundings. But she wasn't bothered about the coming operation, hadn't been since she'd woken this morning.

The trolley was moving very fast and the nurse holding the drip of glucose and saline was almost running to keep up.

'Nothing worse than dehydration for the skin,' Jeremy had said when he'd visited her early that morning, long before the nurses had been due in to prep her for her op. He'd set up the drip himself. There had been the faintest prick on the back of her hand as he'd slid in the needle.

'You shouldn't be doing this,' Veronica had murmured. 'You've enough to do.'

'I want to do everything in the world that I can for you,' he'd said, as he'd connected the needle to the drip giving set.

'Feeling nervous?' he'd asked.

'Not a bit,' she'd said. 'But, then, I never thought that I would once I put myself in your hands.'

He was sitting on the edge of the bed, his head bent over her hand. His black hair gleamed in the early morning sunlight shining through the east window. She reached out her free hand and ran her fingers through it.

'Oh, Jeremy, I do love you,' she said softly. 'I wish there were more words to express how I feel.'

He moved round to the other side of the bed to avoid the drip stand and, perching on one hip, leaned over her and brushed his lips across hers.

'Love you, too,' he said, his lips wandering over her eyelids and forehead and down her throat to where the top button of her silk pyjamas held her jacket together, forming a deep V between her breasts.

He drew in a long breath and raised his head. 'Not now, I think,' he murmured, planting a kiss on her nose. 'I dreamt about you last night.'

There was a glint in his dark blue eyes that made her ask, 'Was it a sexy dream, or a prim and proper one?' Her smoky grey eyes devoured him. 'Was it sexy?' she repeated.

'Very. You were wearing a grass skirt and a rose in your hair, and precious little else, and you were coming out of the sea. Your beautiful hair was streaming down your back.' He stroked her hair with gentle fingers.

'Are you making this up?' she asked softly, running a finger round his lips. 'It sounds like a film script.'

'With a beautiful heroine playing the lead,' he whispered in a husky voice.

He kissed her hand and stood up. 'I must go now, love. The nurses will be coming to prep you in a little while...'

'And you've got to psych yourself up.' Veronica smiled. 'Good luck, my darling.'

She continued to smile after Jeremy had gone, feeling relaxed and happy and, as she'd assured Jeremy, not a bit nervous about her forthcoming operation. It was as if, once having committed herself, everything seemed right and there was no room for doubt.

Even knowing that it might not be successful, and that it would be a long time before Jeremy could be sure how completely the repair had worked, it didn't shake her composure in the least.

It was three weeks into April, and three days ago Jeremy had pronounced her ready for her operation. Over the last weeks he'd been stuffing her full of a cocktail of vitamins to stimulate and strengthen the skin and nerve endings, which was vital to the success of the op. She'd had a top-to-toe physical by her GP.

'Good general health is a must to ensure success in this sort of repair,' Jeremy had said. He'd thoroughly examined the half-moon area again and had made little marks on her skin where he was going to make incisions or, as he put it, 'Zap away unwanted tissue with a laser beam'.

'Zap,' she said, smiling, 'as in comic-book zap?'

'More or less.' He grinned, and she thought how boyish he looked when he dropped the stern profile.

Aware that his more laid-back attitude these days was mostly due to her, a warm sensation coursed through her, mingled with a little awe—it was awesome to think that she had the power to almost change the character of this strong man and eminent surgeon, who had been nursing her along for weeks.

And now the moment of truth had arrived.

She had expressed surprise when he'd first told her that she was to have a general anaesthetic.

'Because this isn't going to be a short job,' he'd explained, 'and because it's so near your eye, we have to ensure that you don't blink or screw up your eyes. So your lids will be padded down, your hair shaved back to here...' He marked a point about two inches back from her hairline.

Two nurses came in and cut off her musings, and she surrendered herself to their ministrations as they prepared her for Theatre.

Afterwards she realised that she hadn't even flinched when they'd shaved back her hair. Mentally and emotionally Jeremy had prepared her that well. Yet only a few weeks ago she had guarded her scar from sight. Now she wasn't even fazed by the thought that her shield of hair was temporarily to be lost.

I'm half-cured, she thought as the trolley whisked her along the corridor. Whatever happens, I'm no longer obsessed. I can live with this if I have to and not mind people knowing. She closed her eyes and smiled... And all thanks to my darling Jeremy.

Jeremy in theatre pyjamas and cap, making him look even taller and broader, was waiting for her in the anaesthetic room. He bent over her. 'Hi,' he said softly, his blue-black eyes tender.

'Hi, yourself,' she murmured sleepily.

Andrew Sinclair, Jeremy's anaesthetist, was there, too. 'A little prick in the arm,' he said. 'Count back from a hundred for me...'

The weeks that had slipped by as March had slid into April had been strange weeks. April was glorious, full of scents as blossom after blossom opened in the gardens of Heatherington House. Everything was early this year—roses, peonies, lily of the valley.

Veronica had wondered what the gardens around Jeremy's lovely home, The Old House, looked like—she hadn't seen much of it the evening she'd dined there but she'd had the impression of wide beds against a mellow brick wall and had guessed they were a blaze of colour and scent.

Occasionally, she wondered forlornly when she would be invited again, but came to the conclusion that, as she'd conjectured a week or so back, he might well be trying to distance himself now that the day of her surgery was getting nearer. Probably a sensible idea, though hard to bear. The vibes between them were still incredibly strong whenever they were near each other, and they were drawn together like magnets as ripple after ripple reached them.

Sometimes they met for drinks and talked, sometimes they walked across the downs, but except for an almost chaste hello and goodbye kiss they touched as little as possible. Strange, as they had never discussed it. It had just happened naturally, by some sort of osmosis, that this was a wise thing to do…

There were voices a long way off, faint, whispery. Veronica felt herself frown. The frowning hurt, pulling something—painful. There was a noise coming from somewhere—her throat.

'She's coming round…' Jeremy's voice coming closer…closer, tickling her ear. 'Veronica, love—it's all over, the operation's finished.'

She wanted to say, How did it go? But her tongue was stuck to the roof of her mouth and there was something else filling her mouth. A voice said, 'Spit it out, dear.' And the something—of course, it was an airway—was eased from between her lips. Then something cool and wet touched her lips and some moisture trickled inside her mouth. Her tongue moved. She opened her eyes—well, one eye, the other was covered. She focused her one eye on the misty face floating above hers…

'Je-e-r-my.' It came out on a sigh.

Jeremy smiled. 'You're in Recovery, love, next to the plastics theatre, but now you've come round we'll take you back to your room and you can sleep it off. See you later.' He touched his fingers to his lips, but she was already asleep.

* * *

She slept until early evening, deeply at first and then more lightly so that she was aware of people around her, touching her, removing the oxygen mask to clean her mouth. She thought that amongst the murmur of voices she could distinguish, Jeremy's. But the room was quiet when she finally woke and opened one eye wide, remembering that her left eye and side of her face and head were covered in bandages.

The oxygen mask was lying a few inches away, the oxygen fanning lightly across her face. She squinted at the window blinds which were almost closed but filtering through an orangy glow. She was in a half-sitting position, propped up on a mound of pillows.

'Ah, awake at last,' said Jeremy's voice, and he rose from a chair, huge in silhouette against the orange glow from the blinds, and walked toward the bed.

Veronica croaked the first thing that came into her head. 'My arm feels sore.'

'We had to do a skin graft, love, as I explained that we might, so I took it from inside and just above your elbow joint. It will be sore for a few days but should heal quickly.'

She tried to smile to show that she understood, but it came out as a lopsided affair, her mouth refusing to move on the left side.

Jeremy saw panic flare in her eyes. He stroked that side. 'It's all right, my love, it's just residual numbness caused by the battering that the tissues have taken. It'll go.

She tried to lick her lips, but her tongue wouldn't do what she wanted it to.

'Drink?' Jeremy was bending over her, holding a mug. Gently he slipped his hand beneath the pillow to support her head. She gulped down several mouthfuls of iced water and dribbled some out which he mopped with a tissue.

She smiled a quirky smile of thanks and sank back onto the pillows. 'Lovely, you make quite a good nurse. Did you manage to zap it away?' she asked, lifting her stiff arm to her bandaged face.

'Yep, got nearly all of it.' He pretended to fire a gun. 'Zap, zap.' His eyes were full of admiration, he wished he could hug her hard, his brave, beautiful girl. The operation had taken longer than he'd expected and there had been some tricky moments, but he wouldn't say anything about those yet.

Her one luminous pearl grey eye searched his face, bright against the stark white of the bandages. How can anyone look so beautiful, he wondered, after nearly three hours of surgery? 'And was it a success?' she asked, with hardly a tremble in her voice.

He picked his words carefully, though he knew that she would read between the lines. That was always a problem when treating medical professionals—they understood the jargon only too well. What would have reassured a lay person cut very little ice with them. 'The surgery was a complete success, although there might be a bit of tidying up to do later, but, then, I warned you that this could happen.'

The grey eye blinked and refocussed. There was a definite hint of amusement in it. 'Yes, you did, Doctor.' Her speech was rather slurred. 'Poor Jeremy, you can't really tell me anything more, can you? Technically, the operation was successful, but has it done the job? Well, we both know the answer to *that* is that only time will tell. So I'll let you off the hook, my darling, and possess my soul in patience.'

Jeremy kissed the right side of her mouth and traced the left side with his forefinger. 'You're so brave.'

'Not brave,' she murmured, 'simply happy. I've learned

so much through these weeks of preparation that, whatever happens to this outward and visible scar, the inside scar has gone for ever, and that's all down to you, my clever, clever doctor.'

He reddened, and stood up abruptly, and she lopsidedly grinned at him. 'You know,' she said softly, 'I'm starving. Is there any chance of something to eat in this hospital?'

Jeremy worried that Veronica might be a bit too euphoric, a reaction to having got over the hurdle of the operation. It did take some patients that way, and this might be followed by depression. But the next morning when he visited her early before he started work, he found her just as…not exactly euphoric, but serenely happy, in spite of the fact that she must be in considerable pain and her face was swollen and bruised.

According to Night Sister, she had slept well, apart from asking for painkillers at midnight, additional to those she was able to pump through under her own control. She'd been given a shot of pethidine for which she'd been charted, and had slept well after that.

Her morning temperature, pulse and respirations had all been slightly elevated this morning, but not enough to cause concern, and her blood pressure was within normal resting range.

'In fact,' said his experienced night sister, 'I can't recall ever having nursed a patient who has made such a good recovery after surgery. But then, Veronica has the right temperament. I've only met her a few times since she took over A and E, but everyone speaks highly of her.'

Jeremy felt a wave of pride sweep over him. *His* Veronica had the right temperament and everyone spoke highly of her. To enjoy hearing her praised produced a sensation he'd never experienced before.

'I can't stay long, love.' He bent to kiss her very gently, knowing how tender her face must be. 'And I'm in Theatre all day, so I don't know when I'll get back to see you.'

'Ouch,' she said as his lips brushed hers. Her grey eye twinkled at him. 'I'll try to survive, but a goodnight kiss would be welcome.'

'Barring a full hospital alert, that I can promise.'

Mid-morning, when she was sipping coffee through a straw because, surprisingly, her lips had swollen some more, there was a sharp rap on the door, and Alec, looking rather hesitant, opened the door at her invitation.

Veronica's first instinct was to cover the exposed part of her face, which was faintly bruised and tinged a bluey mauve, with her hands, and then she remembered that she wasn't ashamed any more of how she looked and kept her hands round her mug.

Alec seemed frozen in the doorway.

'Alec, how nice to see you. Please, come in.' She gave him her funny smile.

He came into the room, almost, but not quite, closing the door behind him. Always a stickler for professional etiquette, he said, 'I have Jeremy's and Ward Sister's permission to visit, though I understand you must keep pretty quiet for a day or two.'

'Yes, apparently the healing process in plastic surgery is a slow business, and the body just can't cope unless one rests a lot. Almost the reverse of many illnesses nowadays when one can make a quick recovery with antibiotics and so on.'

Alec was still standing a few feet from the bed and Veronica waved him to a chair. He sat down, stiff-backed, and said abruptly. 'And Jeremy tells me that you're going to need several weeks' convalescence.'

'Yes, I'm sorry about that, Alec. He did warn me before I started treatment that I would be off work for a bit, but in my arrogance I thought he was exaggerating and a couple of days would suffice. But Janice is super, she won't let you down, and the nurses are a great crowd. I'll be back before you realise that I've gone.'

He looked at her gravely, his brown eyes warm. 'I doubt that,' he said. 'I'm missing you already—we all are.'

'Oh…' It was a massive compliment, coming from Alec.

He stayed for ten minutes, at ease once Veronica prompted him to talk about some of the cases that had been admitted the day before.

After he had gone, she lay back on her pillows and closed her eye. What a nice man he was, a real gentleman.

Veronica spent the next few days drifting in and out of sleep, too tired even to be bored. Her drip was removed on the second day and she was allowed to get up to go to the bathroom. Her legs felt weak and she was glad of the nurse's arm, though she had thought it unnecessary when it had first been offered. 'It's only a few yards,' she'd protested.

'Nevertheless, you must take it,' the middle-aged nurse had said firmly, tucking her arm through Veronica's. 'Instructions from on high.' And she'd cast her eyes upward, making Veronica laugh.

'I can't believe how exhausted I am,' she confided to Jeremy one evening when he came to say goodnight. 'Is it always like this?'

'For most people, facial surgery is the most draining.

There is so much at stake and the weeks of preparation are tiring. And in your case, peering out of one eye is an added strain.'

He was perched on the side of her bed and their faces were on a level. Veronica leaned forward and touched his cheek, which felt rough with a day's beard. 'And it's tiring for you, too, love, isn't it?' she murmured. 'Waiting to see if your work has been successful. I don't just mean for me, but for all your patients, especially as you get so close to them in the preparation stages. No wonder you put patience so high on your list of virtues.'

He caught hold of her hand and kissed the palm then folded her fingers over it to trap his kiss, as he had got into the habit of doing. It was one of those little love tokens that was creeping into their relationship. They had come a long way in a short time, reflected Veronica with an inward smile, looking down on his bent head, now that the need for distance had passed.

'Yup,' he replied. 'One holds one's breath when one first removes a dressing—not that it gives all the answers, only the immediate one that the wound is clean and not infected and it seems to be holding together. Further healing takes time and it can be as much as a year before we can be sure that we've achieved all that we wanted.'

He'd told her all this before but it seemed to comfort him to repeat it.

'When are my bandages coming off?'

'Tomorrow,' he said, 'mid-morning.'

She didn't sleep well that night, her mind seething with the pros and cons of the situation. Would her wound be all right? Was it clean, and had surgery been successful? It still felt stiff and painful, but that was normal. The bruising was beginning to fade, to khaki rather than black and blue, and her lips had returned to normal.

Her prayers that everything would turn out all right were more for Jeremy's sake than her own. Of course she wanted the op to have been a success, but was prepared to accept it if the results were disappointing, whereas Jeremy would be devastated.

It must always be difficult for him, that first sight of a wound. He had said as much, but, impersonal as he would try to be, she knew that removing her dressing would be rather more of a challenge. He wanted desperately to make up for what he still saw as a dereliction of duty all those years ago in Greece.

Janice called in the next morning as she was going on duty. 'Heard you were going to have your bandages off…'

'How on earth did you hear that? Jeremy only told me that late last night.'

'Well, that's the word on the grapevine. Mind you, Jeremy and the boss were in cahoots over something yesterday afternoon. Perhaps it was mentioned then and they were overheard.'

Veronica said in a dry voice, 'Is nothing sacred?'

'In this place, not a lot.' Janice laughed. 'Anyway, I just came in to wish you luck. Hope all goes well this morning and, please, please, hurry up and get yourself back to work—A and E misses you, I miss you and the boss definitely misses you. We'll all fall to pieces if you don't put in an appearance soon.'

In an uncharacteristic show of affection, she blew a kiss from the doorway and whisked herself out into the corridor.

'Idiot,' said Veronica to the closed door, but a warm glow washed over her at the genuine affection expressed by Janice.

They had certainly grown close over the last few weeks,

when Veronica had used her as a sounding board, discussing the points raised by her progress meetings with Jeremy. He had been right about needing a personal contact to talk to, and Janice's common-sense comments had been cheering and helpful.

She couldn't eat breakfast, and barely tasted her coffee as she watched the hands of the clock creep round. Barring accidents, Jeremy had said, he would be in with his registrar and surgical nurse to remove the bandages at ten-thirty.

At twenty past ten there was a tap at the door and it was opened a fraction.

'May I come in?' asked Jeremy's voice. 'Just me?'

Veronica's heart performed a rumba. Something had gone wrong, he couldn't remove the bandages for some extraordinary reason and he had come to tell her himself so that she would be prepared before his team came...

'Come in.' Her voice cracked.

He strode in, straight to the bed, and stood looking down at her, his face set in stern lines, his dark eyes unreadable. He picked up her hand and pressed it to his lips.

'Veronica, darling, will you marry me?'

It took several deep breaths from the bottom of her diaphragm to get herself under some sort of control before she could speak.

'Jeremy, love, we've been through this before. Don't let's rush things, let's wait until—'

'*No!*' he thundered, and then more quietly, 'No. That's the whole point. I want you to be my wife, I want to take care of you, cherish you, whatever the outcome is of this.' He touched the left side of her face. 'There's no reason why it shouldn't be fine, but I don't want you backing out of marriage because you think you'll look hideous or some such nonsense.'

She'd got herself quite under control now, and said softly, 'I wouldn't do that, not any more. I'm no longer the awful spoilt brat of thirteen or the artificially composed woman of a few weeks ago. I've done a lot of soul-searching since I started treatment and, thanks to you, my dearest, darling Jeremy, I think my last hang-up has gone.'

Then she did what he had often done to her and cupped his face in both her hands. She brushed a kiss across his forehead as if to wipe away the worry lines. Then she kissed his nose. 'Nice nose,' she murmured. Her thumbs massaged the corners of his eyes and she kissed the lids. 'And eyes to drown in, and your mouth…' She gave him a lingering kiss. 'You have a beautiful mouth.'

His guarded expression fell away and a whole range of emotions flickered across his handsome face. 'But will you marry me?' he whispered, dropping to one knee beside the bed.

'Yes,' she said softly, 'I'll be honoured to marry you, my dearest love.'

# CHAPTER ELEVEN

SUE, Jeremy's surgical nurse, carefully unwound the long bandage that had secured the dressing in place since the operation and dropped it into a receiver.

Jeremy stepped forward and bent over the bed. Veronica looked up at him. His face was impassive, it was unbelievable that he had asked her to marry him and she had accepted only ten minutes before.

She drew in a wobbly breath. Had it really happened? Yes, it had, quite definitely. Yet here he was, bending over her, close enough for her to breathe in his particular masculine scent mixed with antiseptic, cologne, soap and faint sweat, every inch the doctor. In one hand he was holding a pair of forceps, ready to lift the dressing, and in the other hand another pair of forceps with a swab of moistened gauze held between the pincers.

'I want you to keep your eye closed when I lift off the dressing,' he said in an even, totally neutral voice. 'And try not to screw it up.'

Veronica knew that he was nervous because he'd admitted that he always was when they first inspected an operation site, and now she knew that his registrar and nurse, were—if not nervous—tense and holding their breath.

This plastic-surgery business, she thought, is real teamwork. She herself was feeling amazingly, deliciously calm—a different calm to that with which she had woken that morning, a calm that had enfolded her the minute she'd agreed to marry Jeremy. She felt safe and secure and brimming over with happiness. 'I want to cherish you,' he'd said.

She smiled inwardly, looking forward to being cherished by Jeremy, for ever and ever.

The room was very quiet as they all waited for him to remove the dressing. It was the moment of truth to which they had all contributed. For just as she had been waiting for weeks since she had started preparing for treatment with those long conversations with Jeremy, so had they had been following her progress.

Preparation is everything—that was virtually Jeremy's mantra.

Trevor, his registrar, had followed her progress because he'd assisted at the operation and Sue because as senior surgery nurse her role had been to make sure that there had been a slot in the theatre schedule for the operation. Now they were waiting to see if their patience and planning had paid off.

Veronica felt the tepid wet swab soaking off the bloodied dressing, and concentrated on keeping her eyelid quite still. The dressing was off! Jeremy dried the scar area with another swab, dabbing it very gently.

There was a concerted releasing of held breaths, and then he said softly, 'Looks good, looks very good.' He smiled down at Veronica, the stern contours of his face softened with relief. 'Now, love, very slowly open your eye. You'll feel it pulling a little against the scar tissue, but Sue will massage in some cream that will soften it.'

It was uncomfortable, forcing her lids apart, and she could feel them dragging at the corner, but Sue worked in some vitamin E cream and it helped, though her eye and the skin round it felt very sore.

'Gosh, that feels good,' she said with a sigh of relief, opening both eyes wide. She smiled a more or less proper smile up at Jeremy. 'Do you think I could see it?' she begged, 'The scar?'

He hesitated.

'Is there something wrong? You said it was looking good.'

'It is, clinically speaking, couldn't be better, but it's red and swollen and your eye is bloodshot…'

Veronica chuckled. 'Oh, Jeremy, for heaven's sake, I'm a nurse, I know what a wound looks like after surgery.'

He looked a bit sheepish, then grinned. He was being over-protective and knew it. 'Of course you do. OK, Sue, out with your magic mirrors, let the lady see our handiwork.'

It was a bit of a shock, Veronica admitted to herself when she looked into the angled mirrors that gave her a clear view of the scar area. It was swollen, discoloured and bruised, as Jeremy had warned, and with her hair shaved back from her temple it wasn't a pretty sight. But experience told her that the swelling and discoloration would subside, and eventually her hair would grow again. And then what? This was only the first stage.

She peered closer. The puckering had gone. Her heart skipped a beat—that had always been the most difficult to disguise, that ugly pleating of the skin. Jeremy must have lasered it away, but cautiously because it had been so near to her eye, then he'd covered it with the wafer-thin skin taken from her arm. Yes—she could just see the edges of the graft where it was stitched to the unscarred skin. The stitches were incredibly tiny.

'I like the needlework.' She smiled at Jeremy.

'Yep, not bad, is it?' he said, blushing with false modesty at her praise. 'Sometimes one doesn't have to stitch—the donor skin can be held in place with a tiny dressing until anastomosis takes place with the undamaged skin—

but in this area the skin is very mobile...' He smiled and their loving eyes met and held, and she knew that he wanted to kiss her...

Trevor cleared his throat and Jeremy straightened up abruptly.

'Congratulations, Veronica, first hurdle over and worth the long wait,' said the registrar.

'It's the other way about,' said Veronica. 'Congratulations and my thanks to you, all three of you. I know what a team effort it has been.'

'We've a long way to go yet,' Jeremy growled sharply, 'so let's get cracking with re-dressing this wound.'

'Where are you going to go to convalesce?' Jeremy asked her when he came to say goodnight. He had drawn a chair up close to the bed and was holding her hand, occasionally bringing it to his lips and smudging a kiss across her knuckles, almost absent-mindedly. It was very comforting, as if it were a gesture grown familiar over many years.

'Convalesce?' Veronica looked blank.

'Yes, love, I told you you would need a few weeks' convalescence before you can think of returning to work.'

'Well, in my flat in Heatherington House. The staff residents' manager said that it was mine as long as I paid the rent.'

He raised his eyes to heaven and said to the room in general, 'Hasn't this woman learned anything?' He smothered her knuckles in kisses. 'I mean convalesce, darling, be mollycoddled, have a bit of TLC for yourself for once, not administered *by* you.'

He leaned forward, his elbows on his knees. 'But you must have a few weeks away. What about this mate of yours, Liz, whom I vaguely remember from school? Couldn't you go and stay with her?'

'She's booked for a film promotion tour so, if you meant what you said about being mollycoddled, that wouldn't be on, and to be honest, I don't think I feel up to travelling as far as Edinburgh.'

'How do you feel about a couple of hours' drive to Somerset?'

'Why Somerset?'

'Because my mum's got a cottage there and does cream teas and knows all about you and very much wants to meet you…though she does remember you from our schooldays. She certainly would enjoy mollycoddling you without smothering you. I think you would enjoy each other's company, you're both independent women.'

Veronica stared at him as if he were mad. 'Are you seriously suggesting that I stay with your mother—my future mother-in-law?'

'That's the idea,' said Jeremy.

'Oh, Jeremy, for a clever man you haven't got a clue. Doting mothers, especially of only sons, are traditionally known to be chary of future daughters-in-law, however suitable.'

'My mum's different, not doting. To illustrate, I wanted her to come and live at my place, but her answer to that was that if she didn't cramp my style then I might cramp hers. She's a good-looking fifty-year-old, has a great sense of humour and down-to-earth common sense. Why not give it a whirl?'

'So she was only eighteen when you were born.'

'Left high and dry by the bloke who had promised to marry her.'

'Is that why you have such a thing about no sex before marriage?'

He shook his head. 'No! When I discovered that women found me attractive, that made me take a long, hard look at sex, love and marriage. I haven't been totally celibate since then, but I haven't dated anyone from the hospital, and I came to the conclusion that when I fell in love, and was loved in return, sex would be put on the back burner until we formalised our relationship.'

Veronica leaned forward and kissed him. 'And what if the woman who returns your love feels otherwise?' she said softly. 'Isn't she allowed a say in the matter?'

He sat very still, his lips against her knuckles, then he lifted his head. 'I rather hoped we might reach an understanding about that. After all, our relationship has been rather unusual, and at this moment...'

'We're in a doctor-patient relationship.' Veronica grinned cheekily at him. 'And to tell you the truth, I don't think I'd be up to fantastic sex right now.'

Jeremy didn't say a word, simply gathered her into his arms and buried his face in her neck.

'You're gorgeous and I could eat you.' he murmured after a while in a muffled voice.

'You make me sound like an éclair,' Veronica murmured as, after a bit more cuddling, he settled her back against the pillows and sat in a chair beside the bed.

'So, about this convalescence—will you consider going to stay with my mother? She really is a remarkable woman and I honestly think that you and she will hit it off.'

Veronica closed her eyes and thought hard. Well, a few days wouldn't hurt and would please Jeremy immensely, and pleasing him was important.

She opened her eyes and smiled at him. 'I'm ready to give it a whirl,' she said, 'just for a few days.'

* * *

She stayed three weeks with Rose Grant, and enjoyed every minute of it. Rose was all that Jeremy had boasted—tall, handsome-looking woman, with stylishly cut short hair as black as Jeremy's, with not a hint of grey, and with the same dark eyes. She was cheerful and competent, with a great sense of humour, and treated Veronica more as a sister than a prospective daughter-in-law.

For the first few days Rose obeyed Jeremy's instructions and made Veronica rest a great deal. To her surprise, Veronica found that she was only too grateful to be shooed off to bed after lunch each day.

By the end of the first week, Veronica found that she needed only a short rest to feel in good form. She persuaded Rose to let her help in the kitchen, preparing cream teas for customers who turned up in droves in the warm sunshine. And by the middle of the second week, she was confident enough to do some waitressing, wearing a chiffon scarf like an Alice band to conceal the cut-away hair, though it only partly hid the neat dressing covering her scar area.

But she no longer minded that being visible, just as she no longer minded Rose renewing the dressing every few days from the supply that Jeremy had left.

They went for a walk most evenings along the leafy lanes with high hedges that surrounded the cottage; the hedges were full of wild honeysuckle and early dog roses. Often they ended up in the village pub where Rose was well known and liked. And they talked, how they talked, with an intimacy and ease that Veronica had only experienced before with her friend Liz.

'I can't believe my luck,' Veronica said one evening when they were walking back from the village. Impulsively she touched Rose's arm. 'To have you for my future mother-in-law. I dreaded meeting you, you know.'

'The feeling was mutual.' Rose laughed. 'In spite of the assurances that Jeremy gave me and the huge build-up of how wonderful you were—are. It was hard to believe that you had changed so much over the years, as he claimed. I was so afraid that Jeremy would be hurt all over again. He had a thing for you when you were both at school, though he tried not to show it. And I know my son, he has an enormous capacity for loving.'

'And so have I—now,' replied Veronica. 'The spoilt little rich girl disappeared a long time ago. I love him, Rose. I'll never hurt him, I promise.'

'God help you if you do,' said Rose lightly.

But Veronica wasn't deceived by her light tone. She means it, she thought, she'd never forgive me if I hurt Jeremy.

Jeremy collected Veronica at the end of the third week. It was coming up to the end of May.

'If I don't return to work now,' she'd told him on the phone, 'I won't want to leave here. It's heavenly and your mother's fantastic.'

She was waiting for him on Saturday morning as he pulled into the drive.

'You look marvellous,' he said, folding her into his arms as soon as he got out of the car. 'What a tan—makes you look like a golden goddess. How on earth did you acquire that?'

'Waiting on tables,' she said gaily. 'Much better than lying in the sun and getting baked on one side only.'

His eyebrows shot up. 'I trust you put loads of sunscreen on… And what were you doing, waiting on tables.

You were supposed to be resting. I have a bone to pick with Mum.'

'Don't you dare. You know what they say about a change being as good as a rest, well, it's absolutely true, I feel great, and it's down to Rose. She's brilliant and funny and makes me feel good.'

'Told you so,' he said smugly.

She kissed him hard on the mouth, with weeks' worth of stored-up passion. 'I've missed you. I want to make love to you so if you're still adamant about not taking me to bed before we get married, please, let's fix the date for our wedding, and make it soon.'

Jeremy looked down at her, his midnight blue eyes full of so much love and desire that they were almost black. They stood in the warm sunshine, their arms twined round each other, their bodies moulded together as one, his hands cupping her neat buttocks. He returned her kiss, his tongue exploring her mouth until she had to jerk her head back to breathe.

She could feel his broad chest expand as he, too, breathed in deeply.

In a velvet soft voice, he said, 'I'm ready to hop into bed with you any time, love, but it would add a bit of extra magic if we could be married first.'

The timbre of his voice made her shiver.

He blew a tendril of hair back from her forehead and followed it with a kiss, and continued speaking.

'Do you remember telling me how hard you found it to break your vow whilst you still had your scar? Well, that's how I feel about mine. Naïve or not, it remains a kind of symbol for me that our marriage will be for ever, not something to be scrapped at the drop of a hat. I'd feel the same if we were entering into a long-term relationship.'

He rubbed his nose to hers and whispered against her lips. 'But I can't wait much longer to carry you off somewhere and make wild love to you.'

'How soon can we be married?' Veronica asked breathlessly.

A car swished up the drive to the visitors' car park.

Reluctantly, Jeremy relaxed his hold on her and tucked his arm round her waist as they walked over to the private entrance to the house.

Rose saw them from a window and flung the door open wide, giving Jeremy a smacking kiss and a hug. 'Lovely to see you, son,' she said. 'I've got to go over to the café and sort something out, but I won't be long. Coffee's perking nicely, so help yourselves.'

'Thanks, Mum.' Jeremy returned her hug and kiss. 'You look blooming.' He held her at arm's length.

'Well, thanks, love, it's all due to the company I've had over the last few weeks.' She gave Veronica a quick squeeze. 'And now I've got to scoot. See you later, folks.'

They went through to the kitchen and poured coffee and took their mugs outside, to sit thigh to thigh on the bench under the ancient, gnarled crab-apple tree.

Jeremy was smiling like a Cheshire cat. 'I don't think that there's any doubt that we'll have Mum's blessing,' he almost purred. 'I just knew that you two would hit it off.' He sipped his coffee and grew serious. 'Now, about the timing of this wedding, where and when, love—any ideas?'

Veronica said dreamily, 'Where… Well, if it were possible, the hospital chapel. I often pop in there for a few minutes' peace when I come off duty. Do they have staff weddings in the chapel?'

'Yes, I've been to a couple there over the years. As

soon as we get back we'll talk to the chaplain about dates and licences and things.'

'OK, I've got the message, you want this wedding as soon as possible,' said Rowland Butler, in his usual breezy fashion. He looked in his desk diary. 'Weddings aren't thick on the ground, but I've some baptisms and blessings to do over the next week. Fancy being a June bride, Veronica?'

June was only days away.

Veronica met Jeremy's eyes. His mirrored her doubt.

'How far into June?' she asked.

'How about June the fourteenth?' Rowland answered with a grin. 'That's if you can organise everything in that time. Most brides need months to prepare themselves.'

'Well, this bride doesn't,' said Veronica firmly.

The whimsical expression on Jeremy's face made her want to giggle. That's just about bearable, it said.

'Don't we have to have a special licence to get married in less than three weeks?' he asked Rowland.

'Leave that with me,' replied the chaplain. 'I'll sort it.'

## CHAPTER TWELVE

'You look absolutely stunning,' Janice greeted her on Monday morning. 'As if you'd been on holiday in the Azores or somewhere hot and sunny.'

'Somerset *was* hot and sunny,' said Veronica with a laugh. She touched the fuzz of strawberry blonde hair growing over the strip that had been shaved away prior to the surgery on her scar—it was just visible beneath the hem of her lacy cap. The crescent-shaped scar itself was covered with a cleverly shaped, skin-toned dressing that Jeremy had prepared for her.

'But when you're off duty,' he'd said, 'I'd like you to remove it and let the air get to it.'

Now she asked Janice, reflecting that before she'd started her preparation sessions with Jeremy she would never have dreamed of asking anyone's opinion on so personal a thing, 'What does it look like?'

Janice examined it closely and then said in her honest, down-to-earth fashion, 'Well, it won't deceive anybody, it's obvious that your hair has been shaved, but it doesn't look unsightly.' She grinned. 'But, then, you couldn't look unsightly if you tried, lucky thing.'

'Thanks.' Veronica was grateful for Janice's frankness and realised how well they had got on together since day one. Over the months, liking had developed into a close, warm friendship. They had visited each other for meals and coffee and she had been welcomed by Janice's family. In fact, their friendship was well on the way to becoming something special.

She had a sudden inspiration. 'Do you think we could get off for lunch together?' she said.

'Well, you're the boss.' Janice chuckled. 'You tell me.'

'Then shall we say, depending on the state of play, we'll take sandwiches outside and eat in one of the courtyards? I've a favour to ask of you, the sandwiches are my treat.'

'Oh in that case...I'd be delighted.' They exchanged smiles and went their separate ways.

In the way that sometimes happened in A and E, the morning was quiet, with only a trickle of patients coming in with minor injuries.

Even on the domestic front it was quiet, and the paramedics brought in only half a dozen patients during the whole morning, and only one of these gave cause for any real concern. An elderly man, George Garret, was brought in with retention of urine. The area over his bladder was as taut as a drum and the poor man was in agony.

'When did you last empty your bladder?' Diana Ferguson asked as she gently tapped his abdomen.

Mr Garret frowned. 'Yesterday I think,' he replied. 'Might have been the day before. I didn't like going, it hurt, and then it just wouldn't come so I didn't drink anything because I didn't want to fill up any more.'

Same old story, thought Veronica. People always stop drinking when their bladders feel full. If only they understood that it was the worst thing to do. The urine sitting there gets even more concentrated and difficult to pass. She usually tried explaining this to patients, but Mr Garret wasn't up to taking in any explanations. There wasn't much doubt in her mind that he had an enlarged prostate, which would have to be removed, solving his particular problem.

She looked at Diana, who didn't seem to be too sure what to do, for although she had gained more confidence as the weeks had passed she was still sometimes stuck for an answer, just as she appeared to be now. She was frowning and gestured Veronica toward the foot of the examination couch.

'I know we ought to catheterise him,' she whispered, 'to make him more comfortable, but he's so frail I'm afraid he might go into shock.'

'Why not give him an analgesic and mild tranquilliser to relax him? Then insert a catheter and, using the slow release method, drain off a little at a time. That should work without sending him into shock. In the meantime, I can ring the GU ward and see if they've got a bed available. They can decide whether to do tests to see if he's got an enlarged prostate, or some other urinary problem.'

Veronica was in her office when Janice put her head round the door and announced that it was one o'clock.

'Oh, good, I'm starving,' said Veronica. 'Let's go and raid the canteen.'

They found a seat in one of the courtyard squares and were silent for a few minutes as they tucked into chicken, ham and salad rolls.

'Sometimes,' mumbled Janice through a mouthful of food, 'the canteen actually rises to the occasion and produces something edible. This is delicious.'

They quickly polished off the rest of the meal and sat back to enjoy their cartons of coffee.

'I'm replete,' said Janice. 'Thanks for the treat. Now, what's this favour you want me to do?'

Veronica tried to stop herself blushing, but couldn't. Now that the moment had come to tell Janice about the wedding, she felt incredibly nervous. She shouldn't be, she told herself. Apart from the busy grapevine, Janice had known for weeks that Jeremy, as well as being prepared to try and do something about her scar, was also special to her, and probably wouldn't be surprised at her news.

She blurted out, 'Jeremy and I are to be married on the fourteenth of June. Will you be my bridesmaid, or matron of honour, or whatever it's called?'

Janice spilt her coffee, swore softly and mopped ineffectually at the coffee in her lap.

Veronica rushed on. 'I know we haven't known each other that long, but I think we've become good friends in the time that I've been here. But if you don't want to be, I quite understand.'

Janice swallowed what was left of her coffee and gave Veronica a hug. 'Don't want to be? Oh, you idiot. Of course I'd like to be—in fact, I will be *honoured* to be your matron of honour or whatever. But June the fourteenth is pushing it a bit, isn't it? There's always loads to do before a wedding.'

They spent the rest of their lunch-hour talking dresses and a shopping spree within the next few days. Janice was thrilled to learn that the ceremony was to be held in the hospital chapel and the reception at Jeremy's lovely country home.

'That's why it's possible to get everything organised so quickly,' explained Veronica. 'The staff at Jeremy's house will do the catering. We're not sending out fancy invitations, we're e-mailing or telephoning friends, or inviting by word of mouth.'

Janice's eyes widened. 'Very twenty-first century. May I tell the staff? There'll be wedding presents and things and a girls' get-together.'

'Well, all A and E day staff will be invited, as well as Jeremy's staff, so the sooner they know, the better.'

'*All* A and E?' queried Janice. 'Including the boss?'

'Especially the boss. He's to be best man.'

'Oh, I'm glad about that. He's OK beneath that iron mask and he and your Jeremy have been friends for yonks.'

*Her* Jeremy! It gave Veronica a glow to hear him referred to like that.

The glow was still with her later that evening when, with Jeremy sitting beside her, she decided to ring her parents to give them the news.

'I need you to hold my hand, darling. We don't contact each other very often,' she said to Jeremy. 'We're poles apart. I'm afraid that they'll only be interested in your…'

'Money?' said Jeremy flippantly, but he gripped her hand hard and brought it to his lips. A mixture of anger and incredulity filled his eyes. 'Poor little rich girl,' he muttered under his breath, thinking of the casual conversations he had with his mother at the drop of a hat. No wonder Veronica had loved being with her.

Veronica nodded. 'And your social position,' she added. And then she surprised herself by saying rather defensively, 'They can't help it, it's just them.'

'Well, we all have our priorities,' said Jeremy, keeping sarcasm out of his voice, 'and your parents have the right to make sure that I can provide for you. Go on, love, make your call now.'

'Bit sudden isn't it—what does this young man do?' asked her father heavily as soon as she'd broken the news.

'He's a consultant surgeon, specialising in plastic facial reconstruction—he's only thirty-two, one of the youngest in the country.'

Her father's voice was lighter. 'Hmm! Plastic surgery—good line to be in. Is he private or NHS?'

'He does both,' Veronica said wryly. 'Now, stop grilling me, Dad, you can have a word with Jeremy in a moment, and he can assure you that he's well able to keep me in the manner to which I am accustomed. Now, please, hand me over to Mum.'

Mrs Lord's voice, usually cool with her daughter who had been a sad disappointment to her, was warm and excited. 'Oh, Veronica, my dear, I'm so pleased for you. This Jeremy sounds...'

'Rich?' suggested Veronica, holding back a giggle and mouthing to Jeremy, 'Well I did warn you, didn't I?'

'Sound,' replied her mother. 'What's his surname?'

'Grant.'

It didn't ring any bells with her mother, who said vaguely, 'I don't know any Grants. Now, where are you being married and who's doing the catering?'

'The hospital chapel and Jeremy's staff at his sixteenth-century farmhouse...he has a cordon bleu cook.' Was Poll a cordon bleu?

There was a pause, then Mrs Lord said, 'That sounds satisfactory. But I don't know that we'll be able to come down for the wedding. We've been invited on a long cruise by some business friends of your father's.'

'Well, let Dad sort it out with Jeremy,' said Veronica, knowing that this was what her mother would want. 'But it would be lovely if you could come.'

Jeremy came off the phone half an hour later, looking haggard.

'I need a drink,' he croaked, and accepted a large whisky from Veronica who had it at the ready.

'I think that your dad more or less approves of me,' he

said, 'and they will be at the wedding. They're going to join the cruise at Marseilles.'

Veronica gave him a hug that nearly choked him. 'I knew that you could do it,' she said. 'I knew that you were a match for Dad.'

The days seemed to fly past and A and E suddenly got busy again as the holiday traffic got into its stride. Veronica, still feeling guilty for taking several weeks' sick leave and knowing that she would soon be taking time off for a short honeymoon, worked hours of overtime to relieve other staff.

She didn't mind being busy because Jeremy was busy, too, and they saw little of each other. He was trying to reduce his waiting list by starting even earlier than usual and finishing later each day. Often their only contact was a telephone call very late at night, though one morning they met early on the bridle path on top of the downs, just as the sun was coming up.

He had ridden the three miles from The Old House and she had walked a mile from Heatherington House to meet at the little dip in the hillside that trapped the sunshine, where they had unexpectedly met months before.

Knowing that this time that she would be seeing Beauty, Veronica filled her pockets with peppermint creams, the horse's favourite.

It was only six o'clock, but the sun was warm. After feeding the handsome horse a few peppermints, Jeremy led her into the little hollow and took her into his arms. They sank down onto the springy turf, leaving Black Beauty to crop the grass.

They caressed and kissed, until Jeremy said breathlessly, 'Control yourself, woman. I'm not made of stone, but I'm not going to break my vow only days away from our wedding. You're not going to have your wicked way with me.'

He rolled over and sat up. 'Now, have you thought where you would like to go for our honeymoon, if you can call five days a honeymoon, that won't take hours of travelling time?'

Veronica sat up, too, and found a stem of long grass to chew on. 'It's the quality, not the time that counts,' she said. 'And as a matter of fact, I have—the Norfolk Broads. Let's do a canal cruise.' She rubbed her nose to his. 'Do you think you are capable of captaining a barge, Mr Grant?'

His voice was dry. 'I dare say I'll manage, but the fine weather might break and we may be rained in for days.'

She smiled dreamily. I can think of lots of things to do on a rainy day on a barge on the Norfolk Broads,' she said softly.

Janice worried about her.

'You'll be worn to a frazzle by the time you get married,' she said, when they went shopping a couple of days later for their wedding finery. 'You should be doing this in a leisurely fashion, choosing your wedding dress, going for fittings and so on, not squeezing in an odd day to find the perfect dress.'

But Veronica, on a high on adrenaline, simply laughed.

'There's a little boutique I've discovered behind the Guildhall,' she said, 'that will fit us both out off the peg, and if any alterations are needed they'll do it on the spot, promise.'

'But we've only got days, and although you'll fit into anything, I'm nearer eighteen than sixteen and they don't come easily off the peg, and I don't want to let you down. And I bet it's pricey, this boutique.'

'Oh, yes, it is,' said Veronica, 'but money is one thing that you don't have to worry about, Jan. I'm lucky, my grandmother left me a nice little legacy so I'm not dependent on my salary. We'll have a whale of a time and splash out on super dresses for both of us.'

They did just that. The boutique was displaying a single, traditional, ivory bridal gown in the window, but Veronica was adamant that she didn't want white, or full length, or frilly. 'I'll know what it'll be when I see it,' she said. 'Let's choose yours first, Janice. Please, say what it is that you like—don't sneak a look at the price tag and reject it because you think it costs too much.'

Janice, who had been planning to do just that, blushed to the roots of her hair, but promised that she would be honest about what she liked. The saleswoman, to her surprise, didn't speak as if she had a plum in her mouth, or seem surprised that she had to find a dress for a size-sixteen, going-on-eighteen model.

'Let's see what we've got,' she said, and began through the rails.

Janice fell immediately in love with the fourth outfit that was brought out for her inspection. It was a mid-calf-length dusky pink silk, superbly but simply cut with a slight flare to the hem, with a matching loose jacket. She tried it on. It fitted perfectly, taking inches off her bust and hips. So that's what good clothes do for you, she thought. Suede shoes and silk gloves in a slightly darker pink were found to match, as well as a pair of pure silk flesh-coloured stockings.

'But no hat,' she said, when the saleswoman indicated the millinery department. 'Hats and I don't go together.'

'I was thinking of a cap of soft red roses,' said the salesperson. 'It'll contrast beautifully with the pink. Do try it on.' She held out the scrap of velvet which was secured by hidden clips.

Veronica was delighted. 'It's stunning' was her opinion. 'I'm not keen on hats either, but this is something else. Tell you what, I'll have something similar, like that...' She pointed to a circlet of pastel-coloured sweet peas, so real-looking that one could almost smell their scent.

'But you haven't chosen your dress yet!' exclaimed Janice. 'It might not go with it.'

Veronica was supremely confident. 'Oh, it will,' she said.

And, of course, she was right. It took her only a few minutes to find exactly what she wanted—a simple ankle-length sheath of honeycomb-coloured tussore silk with a little kick pleat at the hem. It was sleeveless and had a scooped-out neckline, which showed off the golden tan she had acquired in Somerset.

It would have looked too plain on anyone else, thought Janice, but on Veronica, with her crown of strawberry blonde hair, topped with the sweet-pea coronet, it looked absolutely fabulous, enhancing her slenderness to perfection. It was a top designer dress, and looked it.

'Oh, Veronica, you look a dream, out of this world,' said Janice. 'Jeremy won't be able to keep his eyes off you.'

Jeremy rang her at nine o'clock, two nights before the wedding.

'I've just finished operating,' he said, in a voice husky with tiredness. 'Let's go to the Old Thatched Barn for a drink and a snack. Tomorrow night Alec's got something arranged and I can't wait for two days to see you. I'm already suffering from withdrawal symptoms—we've hardly seen each other over these past days.'

They were both so tired that neither of them knew what they ate or drank. 'Something simple and not too alcoholic,' Jeremy ordered. They talked lovingly in slow, short sentences, touched hands when they could and simply enjoyed being together.

By the time they drove back across the top of the downs it was dark, but a midsummer darkness that seemed to hold light in the sky.

Jeremy drew into a layby and wrapped her in his arms and they sat and looked out over the city of Porthampton. As always the hospital stood out like a beacon, with the theatre lights and A and E lights still blazing, and the docks as usual turned night into day under floodlights. The rest of the town was held together by a necklace of orange road lights.

An almost full moon shone on the sea. There was a liner on the horizon festooned with lights, and smaller ships waiting to come into harbour when the tide was right and a berth was ready.

'I feel rather like those ships,' said Veronica softly, rubbing her cheek against his. It was rough with stubble. She added inconsequentially, 'You haven't even had time to shave.'

Jeremy gave a throaty chuckle that rumbled in his chest. 'What's that got to do with you feeling like those ships?'

'Nothing, of course.' She snuggled closer into his shoulder and nuzzled his neck. 'Only because I feel like those ships waiting to come into a safe berth, only I've arrived—you're my safe berth.'

His arms tightened round her. 'I hope you'll always think like that, my love. You must never doubt it. I'm here for you always.'

He kissed her very tenderly on her mouth and then

cupped her chin with his strong but gentle hands. 'You're beautiful,' he said.

'My handsome Oberon,' she riposted.

'Thank you. I believe you.'

He traced his finger gently around her eye. 'And this is looking better every day.'

'I know,' she said. 'Thank you for that, too.'

'Are you happy, Veronica?'

'Yes, very.'

'Then I am, too.' He smiled. 'We need to get moving soon. The day after tomorrow…' He glanced at the clock on the dashboard. It was five past twelve. 'No, tomorrow, we are to be married. We both need to catch up on some sleep before then.'

The chapel ceremony and the reception at The Old House, an eleven-o'clock wedding brunch, passed off like a dream. But, then, it would, thought Veronica, with Alec masterminding it and Janice giving support, and Poll producing mouth-watering food.

'Much like being on duty really,' Janice had said dryly a few days before the wedding, 'The boss directs and I do as I'm told.'

'Gosh, I hadn't thought of that,' Veronica had replied. 'I hope he hasn't been too bossy.'

'No, not at all.' Janice had laughed. 'In fact, it's a nice change to find a man who really seems to know what he's about when talking flowers or laying on cars to take people from the chapel to Jeremy's place. And he's determined that you should get away in good time as you've a long drive up to Norfolk after the wedding. He doesn't leave anything to chance, our Alec.'

* * *

It was early evening when they arrived on the Broads. The narrow boat they were renting was well furnished and surprisingly roomy. The bedroom had a king-size bed in it. Veronica's surprised eyes met Jeremy's.

He grinned and murmured, 'An optional extra.'

They were given a crash course in handling the boat, though Jeremy confessed to having had some experience of narrow boats when in med school.

Alec had sent them off with a hamper made up in his favourite restaurant. Every thing was there, from an expensive champagne in an ice cooler to salmon mousse and sherry trifle.

They tied up for the night in a little offshoot of the river almost hidden by bushes and reeds. A crudely painted finger signpost pointed up the little creek. FOR SALE: MOON RIVER COTTAGE, it stated in shaky print.

'We'll investigate tomorrow,' said Jeremy. 'Meanwhile, let's eat and then test out the king-size bed.'

'Let's do that...' murmured Veronica.

And they did.

WIN $200 WORTH OF HARLEQUIN MILLS & BOON NOVELS!
10 chances to WIN!

Our customers are our most valuable source of information and, in order for us to keep up-to-date in providing you with the latest and greatest of the Harlequin Mills and Boon romance novels, we'd love to read your responses to the following questions.

1. **What is the title of the book you have purchased?**

   ____

2. **What appealed most to you about this book?**
   ❒ Cover ❒ Author ❒ Title ❒ Price
   ❒ Series (i.e. part of a series of books)
   ❒ Other ______________________________

3. **Where did you buy this book?**
   Store name ____________ Location ____________

4. **Why did you choose to shop at this store?**
   ❒ Convenience ❒ Price ❒ Variety/range of books
   ❒ New titles displayed on time each month
   ❒ Other ______________________________

5. **Are you satisfied with the variety and presentation of HM&B books in this store?**
   ❒ Yes - Comments ______________________________

   ____

   ❒ No - Comments ______________________________

   ____

6. **How often do you buy HM&B books?**
   ❒ Every month ❒ Every week
   ❒ Occasionally ❒ Every couple of months

HMB2001A

more questions overleaf...

7. **Do you read other HM&B series romance books?**
❒ Sexy ❒ Medical ❒ Sweet ❒ Special Edition
❒ Historical ❒ Desire ❒ Intrique ❒ Temptation
❒ Intimate Moments ❒ Superromance

8. **Do you read books from our MIRA range?**
❒ Yes - Comments ______________________________
______________________________
❒ No - Comments ______________________________
______________________________

9. **Do you purchase 'New Title News'?**
❒ No, I haven't heard of New Title News.
❒ No, I'm not interested in New Title News.
❒ Yes, I buy New Title News.
Comments ______________________________
______________________________

**The following questions are to ensure we have a true cross-section of our readers.**
Are you: ❒ Female ❒ Male
Your age is: ❒ under 25 ❒ 25–35 ❒ 36–45 ❒ 46+

**Thank you very much for taking part in this survey. Don't forget to fill in the details below for your chance to win.**

Simply fill in the survey, complete your details below and return to: **The Marketing Manager, PO Box 810, Chatswood NSW 2067,** *before the 1st August 2001*, for the chance to win one of ten HM&B book prize packs valued at over $200 each!
Only one entry per person, please.

Name ______________________________
Address ______________________________
______________________________
Suburb ______________ State ____________ Postcode ________
Phone ______________ Email ______________

You may be mailed with offers from other reputable companies as a result of this application. If you would prefer not to share in this opportunity, please tick the box. ❒

HMB2001B